"We don't do well together, do we?"

They should, because they had. But this time it was so different. Her stomach was in knots all the time now, over the prospect of a chance encounter in the hall, or a spur-of-the-moment meeting in the therapy room.

"I'm sorry about that too, Dante. It's my fault. You're my patient, and as your physician I should be doing better by you, but…"

"Then you're fired," he said, his voice totally void of emotion. In spite of his flat words, his eyes sparkled. That dark glint gave him away. Always had.

"Just why would you do that *now*?" she asked.

"Because it's not professional." He moved forward, causing her to step back enough so that her back was pressed firmly to the door.

"What's not professional? My treating you now, with the relationship we've had in the past? Because that's what I've been saying all along, and…"

"What's not professional is what I'm about to do, Catherine. Unless you open that door and run away, what's going to happen between us should never happen between doctor and patient…"

Now that her children have left home, **Dianne Drake** is finally finding the time to do some of the things she adores—gardening, cooking, reading, shopping for antiques. Her absolute passion in life, however, is adopting abandoned and abused animals. Right now Dianne and her husband Joel have a little menagerie of three dogs and two cats, but that's always subject to change. A former symphony orchestra member, Dianne now attends the symphony as a spectator several times a month and, when time permits, takes in an occasional football, basketball or hockey game.

Recent titles by the same author:

A FAMILY FOR THE CHILDREN'S DOCTOR
THEIR VERY SPECIAL CHILD
THE RESCUE DOCTOR'S BABY MIRACLE
A CHILD TO CARE FOR
EMERGENCY IN ALASKA

ITALIAN DOCTOR, FULL-TIME FATHER

BY
DIANNE DRAKE

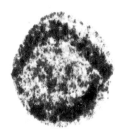

Pure reading pleasure

First published in Great Britain 2008
Harlequin Mills & Boon Limited,
Eton House, 18-24 Paradise Road, Richmond, Surrey TW9 1SR

© Dianne Despain 2008

ISBN: 978 0 263 19897 3

Set in Times Roman 10 on 11½ pt
15-0508-58123

Printed and bound in Great Britain
by Antony Rowe Ltd, Chippenham, Wiltshire

ITALIAN DOCTOR, FULL-TIME FATHER

For Bobby M, an amazing race-car driver
and the love of a very young life.
You're still sadly missed, Bobby.

CHAPTER ONE

CATHERINE stared at the admission slip, not sure what to do. Or say. A new patient was routine. But one with the name Dante Baldassare was not and, right now, her heart was doing more than skipping a beat or two. Of all the places in the world where he could have gone, why here? Did he know this is where she was working? Was he coming here to torment her, to remind her of things best left forgotten?

She'd read that he'd been injured several weeks ago. But hadn't he gone to the clinic in London? That's what the newspaper had said. They'd flown him there for his rehabilitation after his surgery. So how had he ended up here, in Bern, Switzerland? How had he ended up in the clinic where *she* was medical director?

Catherine took another look at the admission slip, in case her eyes were playing tricks on her. *Dante Baldassare.* There it was, his name scrawled on the papers. After all these years, she still recognized the signature. Dante Baldassare—a new admission by Dr Max Aeberhard. Even though Max was no longer administrator of the medical side of operations here, as owner of the clinic he did still have the right to approve admissions. According to what she was seeing, this was a rush admission. Max had been on call, she had not. His decision, and she wasn't going to question it. After all, Max didn't know their history.

But her decision, had she been the one on call, would have been to send Dante somewhere else.

There was no changing what was already done, though. Unfortunately. Dante was already here and in the process of being checked in as a patient. She'd have to have an awfully good reason to send him somewhere else and a love affair gone bad wasn't good enough.

Catherine slumped down in her chair, trying to blot out the image of Dante already trying to creep into her deepest thoughts, the place to which he no longer had a right to be. She'd seen his photo in magazines or newspapers several times over the past five years, so she knew what he looked like. Better now than then, if that were possible. Rugged, chiseled, darkly Italian-handsome and, according to the photos, improving with age.

That was one thing she'd never deny about Dante—he had the good looks that made female knees go wobbly and turned the heads of both genders. That day in the hospital at their first meeting, when he'd come to her for a consultation on one of his patients, it had taken her heart a full two minutes to calm down, had taken the rush of blood to her face just as long to become normal, before she'd even got down to medical business with him. Then she'd slept with him that night and every night they'd had the chance after that for the next six months. Then…well, she didn't want to think about that now. Not when she should be figuring out a way to avoid the man who was, at this very moment, settling into the Geneva Suite. The reason—rehab after a second repair to a shattered ankle.

A second repair? Had something gone wrong with the first? The medical side of her took over for a moment. She hadn't read anything about that in the newspapers, hadn't heard a word on any of the sports reports she tried so hard not to listen to. So, what was going on?

Quickly, Catherine scanned the medical notes sent in from Dante's previous clinic, but there was nothing noted that indicated what had happened. Naturally, the first thing that came to mind was that surgical complications he might have had could lead to an extended stay here. Which she certainly didn't want. A two- or three-week therapy course was long enough if all went well, but if something else was going on…

"Why are you doing this to me, Dante?" she whispered, as she shut the manila folder and laid it down on her desk.

Because he was Dante, that's why. If ever there was a man who knew how to get to her, it was the one she was bound, by clinic protocol, to go greet in the next few minutes.

Sighing, Catherine placed two fingers to her left wrist to see if her heart was beating as fast as it felt. It wasn't, of course. And the tightness overtaking her throat wasn't really a physical symptom of anything either, unless a reaction coming from seeing an ex-fiancé after so many years had a medical name attached to it.

"Just being silly," she whispered. "That was another life. He's over you, you're over him." Empty words. They didn't make the panic rising in her go away. If anything, her symptoms increased. Face flushed. Chest tightened. "It was a relationship that should-n't have been. Twenty-four weeks on the calendar that made me a wiser woman." She'd lived two hundred and seventy-two weeks since the last time she'd laid eyes on Dante and had done quite nicely during all that time, thank you very much.

So why was she reacting to him this way now? Since they'd parted she'd been married, he'd been…well, she'd read what he'd been, which was very busy with the ladies. All over the world!

Trying not to conjure up that image, Catherine picked up her phone and dialed her secretary. "Is Dante Baldassare settled in?"

"Yes, doctor," Marianne Hesse answered. "According to the floor supervisor, he's settled in, and grumpy about being here."

Dante grumpy? Now, that was something she'd never seen. "Page Dr Rilke to go greet him. He's been assigned as Mr Baldassare's doctor, so he can have the honor of welcoming him to Aeberhard." While she made up more excuses to keep herself away for as long as possible.

"You're not going?" Marianne asked, sounding surprised. If there was one thing that could be counted on at Aeberhard Clinic, it was that protocol didn't change. They stood on tradition, and while the clinical concept was casual, the overall clinic tradition was rigid. Except this once. But she couldn't help it. She just plain didn't want to see the man, not until she'd girded herself a little better for it.

"In a while," Catherine responded, hedging. "I have a few other patients I need to see first." And supplies to order, and staff review reports to be filled out, and phone calls to return, and patient discharge recommendations to finalize. There were any number of excuses not to go, all of them quite legitimate. Not good, but definitely legitimate.

To be honest, though, she was curious. That annoying little part of her that knew she was about to do something she'd regret was pushing her into it regardless of what she wanted, positively fighting to burst through. Admittedly, she did want to know if Dante would be impressed by her achievement. After all, she'd gone from junior hospital staff to clinic medical director in five years—an accomplishment of which she was proud. But what would Dante think of it? Or would he even care? He was so long out of medicine now, maybe none of *this* world would matter to him any more.

Actually, she still wasn't sure how he'd walked away from medicine and been so indifferent about it—a man with his passion and skill. Of course, she knew how he'd walked away from her. That was probably the easy part for him, considering how he'd walked straight into the arms of another woman, then another, and another after that. A whole string of others, to be frank.

But she'd done well for herself in spite of all that mess. Gotten on with her life, albeit with a little glitch on the marriage front a couple years ago. Three years after Dante and she'd finally connected with another man, so they'd had a brief try together. No children as a result, however, and no particularly lingering impact from one year spent with a man who, one week after their wedding, had declared it was time for his wife to stay home, cook dinner, do laundry and bear him lots and lots of children. Somehow Robert Wilder had missed the fact the she was a career-woman, and somehow she'd missed that fact that her husband's views on the perfect marriage were anything but what she considered perfect. It hadn't worked out, and there really wasn't much to say about it. She'd made a mistake. Robert deserved a woman who could be everything he wanted and she deserved her freedom from a man who wasn't anything she wanted. Which was what she'd got.

Still, the impact of being left out of the important decisions in her marriage, of having someone else make them and not include her in them…she cringed even now, thinking about it.

But the timing of that little detour in her life had worked out as one month after their divorce she'd found herself in a major career change, going from being a lower-end staff doctor in a rehab hospital in Boston to medical director of a rehab clinic in Bern. A sensible move that had made her divorce seem all the better. The only thing that had bothered her some had been keeping Robert Wilder's name. She'd intended to go back to Dr Catherine Brannon, but the whole Aeberhard Clinic offer had come so quickly, and her move to Switzerland almost in a whirl-wind, then the ensuing months had been so busy she'd barely had time to breathe. So all her legal papers were still in her married name, but getting everything changed back to her maiden name was definitely on her to-do list when she had time. Right above taking that long, uncomfortable walk to the Geneva Suite to greet their new patient.

The phone buzzed, and Catherine jumped like a skittish cat.

"Dr Rilke isn't here yet," Marianne informed her.

"Where is he?"

"He's on his way. Says he'll be here in fifteen minutes. And we don't have another doctor in the building at the moment."

A long, quiet pause on Marianne's end spoke the words the woman did not say. It was Catherine's responsibility to go greet Dante. Catherine knew that, and her secretary knew that. Of course, Marianne wouldn't say it, but she didn't need to. "If he's not here in fifteen minutes, I'll go and see to Mr Baldassare."

"Very good, doctor," Marianne said, clicking off.

Catherine leaned forward, studying the outside of Dante's folder. She was drawn to read more about him, and her fingers even skittered their way across the desk, latched onto the folder and pulled it back towards her, inch by inch, across the glossy mahogany top. She'd already read the routine information— height just over six feet, weight one hundred and ninety pounds. "You haven't changed much," she whispered, still refusing to take another look, specifically at the line indicating spouse. The truth was, she didn't know. The bigger truth was, she didn't want to know. She'd seen that he still lived in Tuscany. She'd also seen that he listed his occupation as race-car driver. *Not medical doctor.* But she hadn't looked at anything filled in under family.

Her fingers played across the top of the file and just as she'd decided on pushing it away so she wouldn't be so tempted, Marianne buzzed.

"Dr Rilke just called in."

"And?"

"He's stranded. Car trouble. He said he'll call for a mechanic and be in as soon as he can, but that it won't be for quite a while."

Catherine balled her fist and gave a little slam to Dante's medical folder. Now she'd have to go and see Dante. No getting around it. "Ask him if we could send the clinic car to fetch him." A suggestion made from sheer desperation, and a rather pathetic one at that. But desperate times called for desperate measures... Catherine knew all about that.

Something else she knew was how silly she was being about taking a look in the folder. She was the medical director here, for heaven's sake. It was her duty to know her patient. Her duty to know every patient in Aeberhard Clinic. After all, she could practically recite Mr Newlyn's family tree by heart, and call off the last four surgeries performed on Mrs Rakeen. She knew the names of Mr Gaynor's three grandchildren and had intimate details of how to contact each of Mr Salamon's four ex-wives. All from studying the charts. So this was ridiculous, thinking of Dante as anything but a patient.

Opening her balled fist, Catherine flipped back the cover of the folder and began reading. The first page was chock full of all the routine information she'd read before. The second page was about Dante's medical history, which she'd also read earlier. Most of it sketchy, though. At the very bottom her eyes caught on the section where Dante had listed past surgeries. Appendectomy ten years previously. Damn, she didn't want to remember that. Not the surgery itself, but the scar. How many times had she kissed that scar?

Fighting back that image, she kept on reading. More routine facts, financial information connected to how he could cover his bill, that kind of thing. Then, on the last page, she came to what she hadn't wanted to read—family contact information. Not that she cared if Dante was married, because she didn't. Yet it felt funny. An intrusion to which she wasn't entitled. Or one that would dredge up some of the plans they'd made that would have put her name there on that page as his spouse.

"Stop it," she whispered, drawing in a steadying breath. "One ex-fiancé pops up and look how you're acting." Her heart hadn't even skipped a beat six months ago when Robert had called to ask her to sign a property settlement document she'd overlooked during the divorce. Yet look what she was doing over Dante. Going positively crazy! And she didn't know why. That's what troubled her. Dante was just another patient...granted, he was one she'd slept with and almost married, but he was still just another patient. She wasn't in love with him. Hadn't been for a good long time. So maybe this was simply an overreaction to the very hard life she was living right now. All work, no play. And no meant absolutely no, none, *nada*, not a drop of play not even for a minute. At least, not in the past year…or past two years, if she counted her marriage.

So, in an effort to prove to herself this silliness wasn't as much about Dante as it was about herself, Catherine forced herself to finish reading the admission papers. The next few lines were all routine information. Same with the next few after that. Then she came to the next-of-kin section, and that's where she stopped. There, in Dante's own handwriting, was the name Gianni Baldassare. Age eight. Listed as Dante's son.

"His son?" she whispered, shaking her head, then going back for a second look to make sure she'd read it correctly. Which she had, and that didn't make any sense at all. If Dante had an eight-year-old son, that meant Gianni would have been three when she and Dante had been engaged.

She'd been engaged to marry a man who had a son, and he hadn't mentioned it? Just like Robert hadn't mentioned his plan for a stay-at-home wife?

"How could he have…?" she whispered, still stunned by the fact that Dante had asked her to share his life but had failed to include her in a very important part of it. She would have been a mother after some fashion yet he'd never bothered to tell her?

Of course, that proved solidly that she hadn't known him, didn't it? The evidence of that was in the photo—one she'd seen published in a sporting magazine a month after he'd gone home to be with his family. Dante in the arms of another woman, while Catherine had still been wearing his engagement ring. Full color, full page, that full Dante smile she'd thought had been only for her while that blonde in his arms looked on adoringly.

Catherine shut the folder, too dazed by what she'd just read to think, and buzzed Marianne. "Any word on Dr Rilke's arrival?"

"Sorry, doctor. I offered to send a car, but he doesn't want to abandon his car on the road. He asked me to tell you that he'd be in once he got his car towed to the garage."

Catherine was seeing the handwriting on the wall now. No Rilke meant she had to go. Had to get Dante settled in herself. No more putting it off. "I don't suppose he knows how long that will be."

"He's hoping within the next hour or two."

Clinic policy was nagging at her now. This was an expensive facility, very small, very exclusive, with the best physicians and the best accommodations in the world. More like a resort than a medical treatment facility. People who paid to be here expected their doctor in attendance immediately. Dante wouldn't be an exception. "Call the floor nurse and tell her I'll be down to see Mr Baldassare in five minutes." Five minutes, five hours, five years…it really didn't matter. She had to do it. That's all there was to it. Once, five years ago, she'd donned sturdy armor when she'd kicked Dante out of her life. Now she only hoped she had some of that armor left over, because one thing was certain. Dante Baldassare did know how to get to her. That was evidenced in the half-moons her fingernails had just dug into the palms of her hands when she thought about him.

"No, I don't want to be here. Why the hell couldn't I have just gone home, put my foot up and healed there?" Spent the mornings looking out the window and afternoons listening to Gianni learn to read. Not a bad way to pass the time during this imposed holiday, as he preferred to think of it.

"You know why, Dante," Cristofor Baldassare said, tucking his brother's suitcase into the closet. "Because you won't heal there. You'll find a way to do everything your doctors told you not to do, and injure yourself again. *Again!* Like you did last time you came home to recover. You've got a good chance to fully recuperate for the start of the next racing season if we let someone else take charge of you."

He gave his older brother a toothy grin. Separated by fifteen years, with Dante the older at thirty-five, the two of them bore no family resemblance to each other. Dante's classically handsome Italian looks, as well as his dark and brooding attitude, were in stark contrast to Cristofor's sunny disposition, fair-skinned complexion and blond hair, a remnant of his great-grandmother's Scandinavian blood. "And I'm not going to be the one to go against Papa on this, Dante. If you want to argue with him about checking out of here and going home, that's fine, you can argue. But I'm staying out of it." He threw his hands into the air in mock surrender. "Your decision entirely."

Dante ran an irritated hand through his hair. Papa's expectations and demands were a force to be reckoned with in the family, especially as his father wasn't allowed to be as physically active since his heart attack, and right now he didn't feel like reckoning with the man. Besides, he understood his father's concern over his condition. One son already dead, and now another one seriously injured. As a father himself, he knew what his own parents were feeling. So, out of respect, he'd go along with this inconvenience for a while, stay here, take a rest, submit to physical therapy.

"OK, so I'll let it go for now. You don't have to go against Papa. But I'm not staying long. A week or two at the most, until I know what I need to do to get full movement back and build up my muscles. Then I'm coming home." Two weeks without Gianni—it was already killing him.

Who'd have ever thought he could get so attached to another person? But Gianni was his heart and soul and the separation was pure torture.

"Let's wait for a week or two before we make any decisions, OK?" Cristofor said.

"We? Since when is this a *we* decision? Have I ever let my baby brother make decisions for me?" Laughing, Dante picked up a spare pillow and lobbed it across the room at Cristofor.

"It became my decision when Papa told me to make sure you do what you're told." He caught the pillow and threw it back. "And I'm not about to cross him, Dante. He's under too much stress already. He doesn't need more."

The pillow hit Dante square in the face, and he threw it right back, but Cristofor deflected it and it went sailing at the door just as the door opened and someone stepped in. A woman...a woman who wasn't quick enough to avert the flying pillow. She took the hit square in the chest, then stepped back, shocked, not injured, clutching the pillow to herself.

Cristofor turned red-faced, while Dante wiped his eyes and forced himself to stop laughing. Then he turned to her to apologize. "I'm..." His voice broke, and he stopped. Swallowed. Drew in a deep breath. "Catherine?"

"Dante," she said, without inflection.

Her voice was the same, yet different. Fuller. A little throatier. "What...? Um...I didn't know you were here." Her fixed stare on him was cool. Not friendly, not unfriendly. Not affected in any way, which surprised him because he remembered her eyes as warm, and the stare she'd always given him provocative. But not now. He stared for a moment, trying to find a bit of the old Catherine, but none of it was there. "I didn't see your name on the literature."

"My name is at the top of the literature, actually," she said, dropping the pillow onto the plush easy chair by the door.

As if to prove her wrong, Dante grabbed up the packet of information he'd been given pre-admission, and took a look at the staff roster. But what he saw wasn't Catherine Brannon. It was Dr Catherine Wilder. Which meant she'd gotten married. He hadn't expected that. Of course, he didn't have the right to that expectation, did he? Didn't have the right to anything where Catherine was concerned. Not even to think of her.

Dante looked up at Catherine again. "I didn't know." And that was the truth. Sure, the fact that he'd be under the care of a rehab doctor by the name of Catherine had possibly persuaded him to choose this clinic over several others, for no particular reason other than a little sentimentality. Yet he'd had no reason to suspect that his Catherine would be the Catherine in the brochure. But, damn, if that hadn't turned out to be, well, he wouldn't go so far as to say good. Maybe interesting?

"And if you had known, would you have chosen Aeberhard?"

He was still surprised by the turn of events. "It's the best in Europe, isn't it?"

"Yes," she answered, "it is."

"Then I would have chosen it." Easy to say, but he wasn't sure. Catherine was good. He knew that. But having the doctor in charge of his medical care falling into the line of past lovers? Well, he'd expected to be bored out of his mind here but, if nothing else, the next couple of weeks should prove to be interesting.

"Small world, isn't it?" she said, shifting a quick glance at Cristofor.

"Smaller than we'd ever guess," Dante responded, also shifting his glance to Cristofor. "My brother," he said, nodding in Cristofor's direction. "Cristofor, this is Catherine Brann—Wilder. Dr Catherine Wilder. We were...colleagues, back in Boston."

Cristofor looked first at Dante, then at Catherine. Then smiled. "He never told us he had such a beautiful colleague," he replied, turning on his typical ladies'-man charm, something that had never, until that very moment, bothered Dante.

"And he never told me he had such a handsome brother," she answered, duplicating Cristofor's charm with a warm smile. "Or, actually, any living brother at all."

Dante cleared his throat. "I don't recall you ever asking."

The warm smile she had for Cristofor went stone cold as she turned to Dante. "Even if I had, would you have told me? You weren't exactly open about things, were you? Open, or honest?"

"Why do I get the feeling there's more going on here than meets the eye?" Cristofor asked.

"The only thing going on here," Catherine stated, "is that, as director of this clinic, I've come to welcome your brother to our facility and to help him get settled in and acclimated. It's what I would do for *any* patient." She was avoiding looking at Dante now, instead fixing her stare on his brother.

"Except I'm not just any patient, Catherine," Dante said, drawing in a tense breath. "No matter how you want to frame it, you know I'm not!"

Cristofor took a long, hard look at the both of them and started to edge his way to the hall leading to the door.

"No," Catherine admitted. "I don't suppose you are just *any* patient."

Dante eased out the breath he'd been holding. "Good, because I don't want our past—"

"Our past is just that. Our past."

"But you admitted I'm not just any patient."

"You're not. You're a celebrity. You can afford our best suite. We've had celebrities before, and we have to take special precautions to keep their fawning public at bay. I'm sure it will be no different with you."

Cristofor finally made it to the door, and as he slipped into the hall, he paused briefly. "Nice to meet you, Dr Wilder. I think I'll leave you and Dante alone to settle this…whatever it is going on between you, and go find myself a cup of coffee."

Before either Dante or Catherine could say a word, Cristofor was beating a hasty retreat down the hall, not even looking back.

"Looks like we scared him off," Dante commented casually.

"Speak for yourself, Dante. You can read anything you want

into this situation, but to me it's strictly professional. I'm the doctor, you're the patient. That's all there is. We'll heal your broken ankle and you'll be gone. End of story."

"Then sleeping together the way we did for all those months, and getting engaged, didn't mean anything to you?" he challenged, not intending to be contentious as much as wanting to evoke something more than ice from Catherine.

She cocked her head, looking thoughtful for a moment. Then finally, she said, "That's right. We did sleep together, didn't we? I guess I'd forgotten about that part of my life."

He opened his mouth to reply, then shut it, and simply smiled. Sizzling, red-headed temper. Beautiful fire in those green eyes. He'd never seen that in her before, but he had to admit, he liked it in her now.

CHAPTER TWO

"HE'S w-what?" Catherine sputtered, not sure she'd heard that right.

"He's requested you to be his physician here. I went in to explain his therapy schedule to him and he said he wanted Doctor Wilder to oversee his therapy." Dr Friedrich Rilke shrugged casually. "Sorry, Catherine, but we do always bow to our patients' requests if at all possible or reasonable. Dr Aeberhard insisted on that when he ran the clinic and I'm sure he wouldn't have that changed now that he's stepped down from admin duties. Dante Baldassare specifically said he wants you to be his doctor in charge so, unless there's a good reason for you not to be, I'm literally handing his chart back to you." Which was what he did.

A good reason? Did she ever have a good reason! "I admitted him, Friedrich. Went down to greet him, said hello, gave him a five-minute explanation of how we do things here at Aeberhard, then left. That's all there was to it. And I don't want to be Mr Baldassare's doctor. I don't like him, I have a full schedule of other patients, and you're much better with ankles than I am. I specialize in knees, for heaven's sake. Did you explain that to him, that you're the ankle specialist?"

"Explained it, and he wasn't interested."

"Do you think you could you talk him into using one of the other staff members?"

Rilke gave his head an adamant shake. "The man was damned insistent about wanting you. He made that perfectly clear, and he threatened to call Dr Aeberhard personally if we don't grant his request." He paused for a moment, looked thoughtful, then finally said what he seemed almost reluctant to say. "Is there something personal between the two of you? He seems almost… proprietorial. Well, maybe that's not the best word to describe it, but he does act like he has some connection to you. And you're protesting this whole situation much more than you should be."

Dante being proprietorial after all these years. Now, wasn't that funny? Like he had the right to be anything where she was concerned! "Maybe it's because I was the first doctor he met here. Patients do become attached, you know."

"After five minutes?" Friedrich shook his head. "I shouldn't think so, but if that's what it is, I'd call it more a fixation. And that still doesn't explain your reaction, Catherine."

"Not a fixation. We worked together briefly back in Boston, years ago. Didn't get along then. But I suppose he's requested me because he knows my qualifications better than he knows yours." It sounded logical, although Friedrich's eyes were squinting, indicating he still wasn't convinced. "He's a very controlling man…" To say the least!

"So, you worked together? How's that? He's a race driver."

Catherine nodded. "He used to be a surgeon." Odd, to say that. *Used to be a surgeon.* On the occasions she'd listened to sports reporters mentioning his name, even then the image of *Dr* Baldassare had not dissipated. Simply a case of her own stubborn mind not moving forward.

"That's awesome. I didn't know any of the Baldassares had done anything other than auto racing."

"You're a fan of the sport?" she asked, a little surprised by that.

He nodded. "And of the whole Baldassare family. They're legends. One of the best race teams in the world. Dante's so close to the title, and after Dario was killed…"

"Dario," Catherine stated. She knew the story. Painful. Sad. Not much was ever said about him, and she understood that. She'd suffered her own losses, which was why she'd never asked questions. Dario Baldassare had died in a race in Spain several months before she'd met Dante, and that's all she knew. Naturally, when Dante's father had suffered a heart attack, and Dante had assumed the grief over Dario's death to be a good part of the reason for it, she'd encouraged him to stay close to his family in Italy for as long as he was needed. That was all part of the story she knew. But the part she hadn't expected had been the announcement she'd seen on a television sports program that her future husband would be staying there permanently and, on top of that, racing for the Baldassare team. That had been painful and sad, too. At least, for her.

Talented man….men," Friedrich said. "Both of them. Such a pity about what happened to Dario. He had the potential to become a legend in the sport. Although Dante is well on his way to accomplishing that himself. "

"I don't like auto racing," she said bluntly. "Not a thing about it." Too many risks, and she hated risk-taking.

Friedrich shrugged. "Then I'd suggest you not mention that to Dante while you're treating him, as he's a world renowned figure in the sport."

"I'm sorry he didn't want you, Friedrich," she said genuinely. "I'd honestly thought you'd pair up well as doctor and patient." She meant that, too. Friedrich was excellent and he had a way about him that wouldn't have let Dante bully him. But that wasn't meant to be, she supposed.

He shrugged again. "You'll do fine with him, but watch

yourself, Catherine. He's got a reputation, lucky man." Friedrich gave a knowing wiggle to his eyebrows, leaving Catherine with no doubt about what the reputation was. She lived with it, after all. And once was enough.

"It won't be long," Dante assured Gianni. "And if you keep asking, maybe your grandfather will bring you here on a weekend holiday." His father, Marco Baldassare, was a tough man. He ran one of the leading race teams in the world and expected strict obedience from his sons and daughters. Even after he'd cut back on his responsibilities, he still worked harder than most men. Tough as nails all the way round, yet when it came to his grandchildren, Marco was a pushover. A real softy. "Just give him a big hug, then ask him."

"Can I stay with you?" Gianni asked. "I can sleep in a chair if there's not another bed. Or on the floor."

"No. This is a rehabilitation clinic. You can stay for a night or two, but that's all they'll allow." Dante truly was sorry about that, too, because he would have loved having his son there with him, but Gianni was better off with his grandparents for the time being. Since he'd adopted his nephew, they hadn't spent too many nights apart, and Dante counted on that stability in his son's otherwise hectic life. Marco and Rosa Baldassare were the stability the boy needed right now.

"Couldn't you rest at home?" Gianni whined. "I can help you walk on your broken foot. Help you use your cane, and get things for you when you don't feel like walking."

"Can't rest at home, not the way I'm supposed to. And they have things here that will help my foot feel better."

"Maybe Papa Marco will bring me *this* weekend!"

"Maybe he will."

Dante and Gianni talked another few minutes, mostly about school work and new friends Gianni was making now that he was living with Papa Marco and Mama Rosa. When the phone conversation was over, Dante clutched the phone receiver another minute, like holding it kept him closer to his son.

He hadn't expected to keep Gianni permanently. After Dario's death, Gianni had gone immediately to live with his grandparents, Marco and Rosa, and no one had questioned that. Then, after Marco's heart attack, Dante had agreed to keep the boy for a while. A few weeks at the most, while Papa Marco had been recovering and Mama Rosa taking care of him. There had never been any talk that Dante would become a full-time parent then, all of a sudden, he had been. It had been a letter from Dario, something that had been misplaced after he'd been killed. In it had been a heartfelt and sad plea from a lonely man who'd just lost his wife, desperately begging his twin to raise his son in the event anything ever happened to him.

So, how could he not? It was his duty to honor his brother's wish but, more than that, it was what he'd wanted to do. Of course, his own parents had expected to raise their grandson, but they had been good about respecting Dario's wishes. And, Dante suspected, a little relieved, considering Papa Marco's new, more delicate condition.

Of course, wanting to raise Gianni and actually doing it had been two different things. His life had been unsettled. At the time he'd wanted to go back to medicine, and had fully intended to. Yet he had been pulled back more and more into the family operation, feeling pressure to step back into a race car and, once again, put the name Baldassare back on the track. With all that going on, then adopting Gianni, it had been a difficult time all the way round. A boy Gianni's age needed a home and stability, which he hadn't had to offer. No stability, no parenting skills.

No Catherine, either. And that was the biggest change of all in his life. He understood why she was having such a tough time with what he was doing. His sister jumped the gun on the announcement that he was returning to racing, giving it to the press before he'd made up his mind. Probably a little bit of Papa Marco's persuasion, he suspected. But what that did was, essentially, to slap Catherine in the face with plans she knew nothing about. So he truly did understand her feelings over that.

He apologized for that gaffe over and over, and believed she'd get over the hurt, and be agreeable. He never, ever considered that she would end the relationship all because he was thinking about racing again.

But she hated racing, and she made that perfectly clear.

Well, she'd made her choice, and after she'd ended their relationship, he'd made his, which was to stay in Italy to keep Gianni closer to the whole family. The boy needed all that support after what he'd been through and, to be honest, so did he. Especially with practically everything in his life going crazy.

Dante did love racing, and he'd been good at it earlier in his life, which was why he ultimately made the decision to return to the sport. Years earlier there'd been reports of a bright future for him in it, yet he loved medicine, and leaving it behind, like he was doing with his plans and dreams for a life with Catherine, wasn't easy. It was a sound choice based on his situation, though. Gianni needed the whole family structure around him, and the Baldassare team needed a Baldassare on the track to maintain its prestige in the racing world. The enterprise supported a lot of people, and at present he was the only Baldassare qualified to race. So the responsibility fell to him to be both father and race-car driver, and he took both of them seriously.

It had been five years since all that emotional strife, and life was turning out to be pretty good. He had his racing, he had Gianni. And the Baldassare racing team was on top, right where they belonged.

Except now he also had this wretched broken ankle being treated by Catherine, of all people, which was a bit of a hitch. He'd get over that, though. In a week or two he'd be back to normal. But in the meantime he could deal with Catherine. In fact, he looked forward to dealing with her. Maybe taunting her a little. Showing her what she'd given up. What she had tossed out of her life.

Catherine…She did look well, didn't she? Better than well, actually. He liked her hair longer, hanging to her shoulders the way it was now. It made her look…soft. Her curves were as good as ever, although he doubted she ever took off her white lab coat to show them off, which was a pity because she'd always been a feast for a man's eyes.

Her husband's eyes now. Sobering thought. And from the look of the sobering little frown lines setting in around her eyes, he wondered if all that conjugal bliss wasn't agreeing with her as well as it should.

Dante glanced down, discovered he was still hanging onto the phone, and finally hung up. Then he gave the blankets a toss and scooted himself to the edge of the bed, fully intent on maneuvering himself into the wheelchair sitting right there waiting for him. It was time to get out of this suite and have a look around. Maybe find Catherine. And do what? He didn't know. They'd had their final arguments years ago, and there was nothing more to say. Or was there? Maybe he just needed to prove a point, to let her know that he'd had a great life without her. A little get-even attitude popping up? He didn't really think of himself as the vindictive sort, but maybe he was, at least where Catherine was concerned, as she'd had the very last word on the death of their relationship, leaving him with nothing to say.

He chuckled. Maybe forcing her to be his doctor *was* the last word he'd been denied all those years ago.

Only thing was, in his intention to go and see Catherine, the transfer from his bed to the wheelchair turned into something a little more daunting than he'd thought, and once he'd managed to pull the chair up next to the bed, he really wasn't sure he wanted to risk the move into it. Not without some stout help who would make sure he didn't transfer himself straight to the floor and another ankle injury.

Irritated with his incapacity, Dante dropped back into his bed and stared up at the ceiling. He wanted to get out of there. Wanted to get the hell out of there. Wanted to get away from Catherine, forget about her again, go back to his real life. Him and Gianni. And his family. No one else!

"Going somewhere?" Catherine asked, stepping between the wheelchair and the bed.

Dante opened his eyes slowly. "Is that meant to be funny?" he snapped. "You know damned well I can't go anywhere."

"Another good mood, I see. Is that the way you're going to act the whole time you're here?"

"Aren't doctors supposed to be compassionate?" he cracked back. "Have a pleasant bedside manner?"

"Ask yourself that question, Dante. You used to be one, didn't you?" She dropped the clipboard holding Dante's medical notes onto the table by the bed then moved the wheelchair closer.

"Now what?" he grumbled.

"X-ray. I want to see what I'll be working with. Other than a grumpy patient."

He heaved an impatient sigh, one clearly meant to be heard. "Maybe I should have let that other doctor work on me. You know, the one who wanted an autograph for every member of his family—all seventy-seven of them."

Catherine laughed. That did sound like Friedrich. "He's a fan," she said, her voice finally softening. "Probably knows more about you than you do."

"Fans to do that."

"And you like having fans?" she asked. "I always thought you were a private person."

"Fans are a necessary part of the job." He sat back up. "You can't get away from it. You take a job where the public gets involved in some manner, and that's what happens." Then he looked at the wheelchair again. "Do you expect me to get into that all by myself?"

She shook her head. "As much as it might do my heart good to see you fall flat on your face, I do have one of the physical therapists on his way to teach you how to do it on your own. You should have it down by this afternoon, then I'll give you your daily schedule."

"My daily schedule?"

"Therapy, regular exercise, meals. Times available to you for things like the hair salon, the spa…"

"Excuse me, but I came here to recover from an accident, and to have therapy."

"Which is what will happen in due course."

"But all the other things…that's wasting my time."

"Didn't you read the brochures, Dante? We have a fully integrated treatment plan here. You know—mind, body, spirit." Her mouth twisted into a devilish grin. "We'll even do skin exfoliation if you need it."

"Except I don't need my skin exfoliated," he snapped. "Don't need spiritual enlightening or anything else that's not about my ankle. What I want, *all I want,* is to get myself over this, and get to the place where I can take care of myself at home. I'm not here on a holiday and, quite frankly, Catherine, I'm surprised you'd even subscribe to this kind of frou-frou medicine. Back in Boston—"

"Back in Boston was another lifetime, Dante. Things change. People change. *Relationships* change."

"I thought you were a better doctor than that," he retorted.

"Once upon a time I thought you were better, too. But we all make mistakes." She stepped aside as the therapist, Hans Bertschinger, came into the room, and she stayed there while Hans started the first instruction on how to get from the bed to the wheelchair. Watching Dante swing his good leg over the edge of the bed, Catherine noticed his hideous hospital gown creep up, and didn't avert her eyes quickly enough to keep from seeing a generous portion of his leg and thigh. Nice, muscular. She did remember how he'd always been in good shape. Sexy, provocative body. She'd memorized every inch of it and never forgotten.

Before the blush set in, she turned away. "Order him pajamas with pants from the gift boutique!" she instructed Hans, then left the room. Once she was in the hall, she drew in a stiff, deep breath, hoping it would combat her wobbly legs, then she teetered her way back to her office.

This wouldn't do. These feelings, these memories…wouldn't do at all. "Get Dr Aeberhard on the phone for me, will you?" she asked Marianne.

Time for a holiday. She'd been here well over a year now, without a single day off. Surely Max would grant her a few days away. While he didn't oversee the medical end of the clinic, he did still run the business aspects, and her taking a holiday was definitely a business aspect. But she needed a few days to go and hide somewhere, and figure out what to do. Figure out how to avoid Dante. How to avoid even thinking about him.

"I know you haven't had a day off, and it's a very reasonable request. Just not right now, Catherine. I'm sorry. If you'd asked a month ago, or a week ago…" He shrugged. "You deserve the time off, and I don't begrudge you a nice holiday, but Aeberhard Clinic needs you here at the moment."

Dr Max Aeberhard—jolly, plump, lots of white hair, white beard down his chest, walked with a slight limp, always a smile on his face. She adored the man, both as a friend and mentor. She'd called him, and he'd come running. He always did. In semi-retirement now, Max still took a few patients for consultation, as well as overseeing the business side. Of course, his version of semi-retired ran circles around most people's version of full-time employed. The man loved his clinic, loved his patients, and he would never completely retire from any of it. It was as much a part of him as was that twinkle in his blue eyes.

"Just a couple of days, Max. That's all I need." It was pointless arguing with him. Max was a kindly man, but once he set his mind to something, it couldn't be budged. She wasn't going to get her holiday. No time away from Dante, not even a few days to collect her wits. In fact, it was because of Dante that she had to stay.

"Do you know how many enquiries I've had already regarding having Dante Baldassare as a patient here?"

Not as many as she'd had. Worldwide sports journalists had been calling almost from the moment Dante had arrived. They wanted interviews, pictures. They wanted to know more about the clinic. At the very least, all the publicity was going to throw the clinic into the center of attention for a little while. She realized that. And didn't want to be a part of it—not on Dante's account, anyway. "We can ignore them. I've already instructed the staff not to mingle with anyone from the media, not to grant interviews, pose for pictures, get caught where any patient or clinic information might be revealed. And I've doubled security on the grounds. As far as I'm concerned, we're braced for just about anything, and if there is a need to give an official statement to anyone, in all reality you should be the one. So everything's taken care of and I truly don't need to be here." Good argument, but she wasn't going to win it.

Max chuckled, his beard bobbing up and down. "Maybe it's taken care of, from your perspective anyway, but they won't ignore us, Catherine. Mr Baldassare has a following all over the world, and all that's come knocking on our door for the duration of his stay. The people outside aren't going to be content to walk away without something. We're small, and we need you here to make sure we keep our medical focus."

"Then maybe we should find him another clinic, one that's better prepared to cope with his celebrity. The one in Toronto deals a lot with celebrities, doesn't it? And they have a good reputation. I might even know the medical director…"

"This isn't like you, Catherine, backing down from a challenge. Even running away from it. Is there something you'd like to tell me?"

"I'd like to tell you that I'm tired, and I need a short holiday. But I suppose I needn't bother."

"When he's gone and things are back to normal, you can have all the time you need. Even enough for a trip back to the States to visit your family and friends, if that's what you'd like to do. But right now I need you to deal with what's happening here."

So she would stay. But when Dante was gone, would things really go back to normal, as Max thought they would? Or would their new-found celebrity status change matters? New recognition, more demand, maybe even the opportunity to expand as they'd talked about. Catherine wondered about all that for a moment, not unhappy about the prospects that Dante's fame might bring. Perhaps him coming here might count for something after all. At least, that's what she wanted to tell herself. "Fine, when he's gone I'll take my holiday. But I think that since he's so famous, you should be the one assigned to his care. It's your clinic, your reputation, your good name…"

"If I didn't know better, I'd think you were trying to avoid the man." He arched his bushy white eyebrows. "Eh?"

"OK, so I used to know him. A long time ago. And I don't think it's good form to treat an old…acquaintance."

"Except your old *acquaintance* requested you specifically, so I've been told. I think we should honor his request, don't you? After all, the goal of Aeberhard Clinic is to accommodate its guests."

"And I think we should maintain a professional appearance here and take me off his case. I'm not comfortable…"

"Not comfortable giving the patient what he wants? Or needs?" Max shook his head and clucked his tongue. "This isn't *sounding* at all like you, Catherine. Not at all. And don't give me the excuse that you're tired, because that's not what this is about."

She liked Max. Actually, in the short time she'd known him, she'd come to love the man like a father. In fact, years ago, when she had still been a medical intern, she'd moved heaven and earth to get to one of his symposiums. Dr Maximilian Aeberhard had been the best rehabilitation specialist in the world, and the instant she'd learned he was coming to Boston she'd finagled a spot in to hear him lecture. doctors from all over North America had been there, and she, a lowly intern, hadn't been granted admittance. So she'd volunteered to be an usher that day, to escort other doctors to their seats. In exchange, she'd tucked herself into a nook at the back of the lecture hall and listened to the most brilliant doctor she'd ever heard.

Amazingly, she'd bumped into him in the elevator later on that day and, for whatever reason the gods had ordained, had been fortunate enough to take tea with him. Then they'd shared an evening meal at his invitation. The gods smiling on her again. After that she'd read everything he'd ever published, practically memorized every text he'd written, and eventually settled into a medical practice chocked full of Max Aeberhard teachings. Life had been good, she'd been advancing. All of a sudden, out of the blue, she'd received an invitation to come to Bern to be interviewed for a post at the Aeberhard Clinic.

Naturally, chances like that didn't come up every day. Didn't happen in most lifetimes. In fact, she'd firmly convinced herself it was some kind of a mistake until the day Max's secretary had called to confirm her appointment. Then she'd had to pinch herself over and over to make sure it wasn't a dream.

She'd come for that interview, of course, not even knowing or caring what kind of post it was. To be honest, she'd have been happy ironing his surgical scrubs, if that had been the position being offered, because it would have put her closer to the man she idolized. But as it had turned out, the post had been Max replacing himself as medical director in order to cut back on a few of his duties—a position for which she'd had absolutely no qualifications whatsoever. She'd walked away dejected and somewhat mystified that she'd received the invitation. By the time she'd returned to her room at the hotel, she'd convinced herself the invitation had been a mistake and Max's interview merely a polite formality on the way to rejecting her. But then the phone call had come. He'd invited her to supper, and that's when he'd made the offer.

Since then she'd asked him at least a dozen times, why her? Why not someone with more experience, more administrative qualifications, someone already working at the clinic who was familiar with its procedures? Dr Rilke would have been brilliant! All she'd ever got out of him, though, had been that he preferred to keep his reasons to himself. So she'd never pursued it any further.

Yet here she was. Medical Director of the Aeberhard Clinic. Living a dream. And the best part was that while Max had turned into a good-hearted mentor, he really did let her supervise the medical practice with almost no interference. It was still his clinic, though. No mistaking that. Otherwise she'd have written herself off the roster for a few days, made arrangements to be replaced, and gone away. Or, more like, run away.

"Did you know that Dante is a surgeon?" Five years out of practice maybe, but that didn't take away his license. He still had claim to the title and, somehow, she still had a hard time seeing Dante as anything but a surgeon. And a very good one at that.

Max shook his head.

"We were medical colleagues. Had some…differences. I'm not sure I can be objective in his care."

"And you're not going to tell me about these differences?"

She shook her head. "Nothing important." To Dante, anyway.

"Well, something suggests they weren't professional. But I'm not going to pry into your *affairs*, Catherine."

She shot him a caustic glance, but didn't reply. Didn't have to. The grin concealed under that beard told the story. Wily old Max Aeberhard knew everything. Or had a keen suspicion. Damn it! She hated being so transparent. "So no holiday? And I don't get to get off his case?"

"That about sums it up."

Catherine thought about it for a moment, then frowned. "I'll accept that. But if I come to you, Max, and tell you that for the good of my patient, or the clinic, or my own personal sanity, you *absolutely* need to pull me off Dante's case and let someone else take over, I expect you to do that."

Max stood, adjusted the suspenders holding up his brown tweed trousers and headed for the door. "I'll accept that, Catherine." Then he gave her a wink. "But I think you need to do some soul-searching over someone who has you so bothered." As he passed her he gave her an affectionate squeeze to the shoulder, then he was gone.

And she was definitely bothered.

It was late morning before Catherine returned to Dante's room. Hans called and reported that Dante was doing fine, transferring himself into his wheelchair, so now it was time to have a look at what was going on with Dante's ankle. He'd had surgery too many times. Had pins put in. Muscle repaired. Tendons sewn back together. A real mess, and the man wanted to get out of there and drive again. He'd be lucky to walk out without drastic assistance.

"I'm going to X-ray, then I'll be taking Dant— Mr Baldassare on the grand tour," she reported to Marianne on her way out. "Screen my calls, will you? If they're medical, forward them to my cellphone. If they're anything else, take a message."

"I've had five in the past hour, requesting—"

"I know. An interview with Mr Baldassare."

Marianne nodded eagerly. "He is so handsome, don't you think?"

To a dreamy-eyed girl in her early twenties, like Marianne, of course Dante was handsome. *She'd* been that girl not so long ago. A little older perhaps, but still with the same dreamy-eyed feelings. No doubt there'd been a good many of them since her. More than she'd seen in those photos at various times. Apparently, there'd been a good many before her, too.

"He's a patient." Catherine struggled not to sound too affected. "I don't notice handsome on patients. It's not appropriate." Such a huge lie where Dante was concerned. She only hoped Marianne didn't see the look in her eyes. Dauncy, her mother called it. *You lie to me, Catherine, and I can always tell. You get that dauncy look in your eyes.* Catherine blinked twice on her way out the door just to make sure anything dauncy that might be there was washed away.

Dante was actually sitting up in his wheelchair when she entered his room. Wearing pajamas. A richly embroidered silk robe covered them. Not at all Dante, she thought. He slept in the nude, put on a T-shirt to be modest. No pants. Never covered his splendid backside with anything. How many mornings had she awakened with a good dose of Dante padding across the carpet, her stare fixed on that backside? That, along with a cup of coffee, had been the perfect way to start the day, especially when he'd come back to bed to take care of the mood he'd always put her in.

There she went again! Just one look and she was off on another fantasy. Which she could ill afford, and didn't want happening.

"You look like you've seen something awfully pleasant," he commented. "Anything I might want to know about?"

"Don't mistake my bedside manner for anything personal,"

she warned, trying to sound professional when her skipping heart was anything but. "I'm always pleasant with my patients."

"Except me."

"You can certainly request another doctor, if you're not happy with me. The owner of the clinic himself is available. He's the finest rehabilitation specialist in the world, a very pleasant man, and I'm sure he'd be able to fit you into his schedule."

"When did you become so uptight, Catherine? You used to have a spark about you. An eager optimism. You always smiled, yet I haven't seen you smile since I've been here, and that's a pity with your beautiful smile."

"You haven't earned the right to comment on my smile, Dante." Her voice was so chilly it swept out of her on shards of ice. "Or anything else about me except my professional abilities."

Naturally, he commented on that. "See what I mean? You're uptight. Stiff. You don't find any pleasure in your life, and it's going to make you very old, very fast."

"You don't know me well enough any more to say those things." Catherine stepped in behind the wheelchair, giving it a sharp nudge towards the door. "We had six months together, and in those months we never even…" Got to know each other. Got to be honest. "We were merely satisfying certain biological urges for a short period of time, and that's all there was to it. We mistook hormones for emotions and thought that was enough to make a marriage."

Dante laughed. "Hormones aren't necessarily a bad way to start a marriage."

"I'm not surprised you'd think that." Although, with the chemistry they'd had between them, he wasn't altogether wrong.

"Do you ever think about us, Catherine? Over the years, have you ever wondered what it might have been like if things had worked out differently?"

She had, on so many occasions. But she wouldn't tell Dante that. "No. When it was over, I moved on." Like he had, only he'd moved on even before it had been over. "No point in lingering over something that wasn't meant to be."

"Was I that despicable a lover?" he asked. "I thought I satisfied you, gave you what you wanted. I thought we were good together."

"In bed, we were fine. *You* were fine. I had no complaints that way." Just as they reached the hallway door, Catherine stopped pushing the wheelchair and spun it part way around to face her. Then she bent down to him. "But sex is all it was. Something convenient in two hectic lives. It happened, it ended. We've moved on. So, please, be enough of a gentleman to let it go. That will make your stay here much easier...on both of us."

"I never meant to hurt you, Catherine," he said, his voice suddenly dropping to a whisper. "I told you that every time I called. What happened to me wasn't what I'd expected in my life. It was a difficult time."

"Was it, Dante? Was it really?"

Briefly, he looked at a loss, but that passed all too quickly. "You don't know a damned thing about it!"

"Don't I? Because what I seem to recall is that you left medicine and became a race-car driver. People don't just do something like that, Dante. You know, go to medical school all those years, become a surgeon, then drop all that to spend your life driving around a race track. And, oh, by the way, forget to mention that to the person they intend marrying."

"And I did apologize for that. Besides, it's not like you didn't know my family was in racing. That I'd had a brief try at it when I was younger."

"And your brother was better, but that was fine with you because your true passion was medicine. You told me all that, Dante. Silly me, I believed it."

"My father needed me. My *family* needed me."

"They needed you to make a worldwide announcement that

you were returning to the sport before you even mentioned it to the woman who thought she was marrying a doctor? Or were you ever really planning on marrying me? Maybe that was just another of those conveniences we had, something to make us feel a little more proper about our relationship?"

"I told you—"

"What you told me, Dante, was that you had to race. That was it. No alternatives in there for me."

"My father was sick, Dario was gone, the entire Baldassare racing team was struggling. At the time I was barely able to get through it, and I coped the only way I knew how. I didn't mean to hurt you, Catherine, but I'm not going to apologize any more because it's wasted on you."

"Yes, it is wasted because while maybe you didn't mean to hurt me, you also didn't mean to think about me through all of it. You left me out, Dante. Totally out. But so you'll know, I wasn't hurt." Such a lie, and she knew, full well, that dauncy look was creeping into her eyes again. "Just a little disappointed, but I got over it."

"Yes, you did, didn't you? You went on and found yourself a magnificent life. You've done well for yourself, and I'm not surprised about that. You were…are…a brilliant doctor. I'm happy you got the life you deserved."

What was there to say about that? Nothing to argue, nothing to snap at. This was a bit of the old Dante, the one she'd never been able to resist, never been able to stay angry with for more than ten seconds. Damn it all, she still wanted to be angry. Wanted to snap at him, to argue with every little thing he said. But he'd just disarmed her, something he'd always been so brilliant at doing. He'd say something like he just had then they'd tumble into bed and…

Catherine cleared her throat. "I need a fresh look at your ankle, Dante. There's a reason why you're not healing as you should, a reason why you're still having so much pain. The old X-rays your doctor in Tuscany sent didn't show anything so I need a new look. With any luck I'll figure out what's going on, and by end of the day have you on a real road to recovery." Then out her door, and out of her life. Again. But for good this time.

CHAPTER THREE

"And the last room on the tour is the solarium." The doors into the room opened automatically, and they entered. Catherine brought Dante's wheelchair to a stop at a mosaic-topped table near the south-facing window, one that overlooked the craggy landscape outside.

While Aeberhard Clinic claimed Bern as its official address, it was actually situated outside the bustling, old-world city, in the Bernese Oberland, a lush area of Swiss lowlands, alpine foothills and alpine massif. Aeberhard Clinic was actually close to the massif, for which Catherine was grateful, as she particularly loved this view of it with its vast mountains, accented with cliffs and various rocky shelves.

It was especially a treat for her to get lost in the view of the great spires and turrets jutting up from Deuschler Castle, visible on a cliff in the distance. A small castle as castles went, it was still a private residence, she'd heard, as were many of the other castles dotting the countryside.

Now, with the snow settling in for the season, it was all a breathtaking fairyland. But it was also close to the time of year that so many of the ski injuries they would eventually treat would come in. She wasn't going to think about that yet, however. It was still early in the season and the skiers wouldn't be out for a while.

As she maneuvered Dante's wheelchair so he could feast on the magnificent view that she herself tried to find time to enjoy at least once a day, Catherine noticed he wasn't even looking outside. Rather, his gaze was fixed on the tile floor, his face twisted into a dispiriting scowl. Dante was worried about his condition, she guessed, as well he should be. He'd been that way throughout the tour of the entire facility, pretending interest but, in actuality, far away. Nothing she'd said had really snapped him out of it, and it was crossing her mind now that if this had been his normal state since his accident, he might well need attention for that, too. Somehow, though, she couldn't see Dante giving in to depression. He was too strong-minded, too demanding of himself to stray off course.

But she hadn't known him for a very long time now, had she? Things did change with people. She was a walking, breathing testimony to that! "We serve tea in the solarium every afternoon," she said, taking her place next to him at the table. "It's not required, of course, but we do like to give our guests a chance to unwind after the day and indulge in something that's more traditional than medical. It works wonders for the psyche."

"Guests? Psyche?" he snapped suddenly. "For God's sake, Catherine. I've listened, *ad nauseam*, to your memorized speech about Aeberhard for the past hour. The spa, the pool, the hair salon, the gift shop, the catered menu, room service…If I'd wanted to go to a resort in Bern, I'd have checked myself into the hotel at Giessbachfälle. It's larger, the amenities better and the beds more comfortable. But I'm not looking for a hotel!"

Not what she'd hoped for, but at least he was talking. It was a start. "Do you take antidepressants?" she asked, the way any good doctor would.

"You know better than that!"

"Actually, no, I don't. In the scheme of things, Dante, I know nothing at all about you except what I'm seeing right now, which is a drastic mood swing." She did know a little bit from the news accounts she'd read over the years, too. "So I'm obligated to ask you, do you take antidepressants or any other kind of medication that could bring about mood swings or personality changes?"

He finally looked at her, made direct eye contact, and stared, unblinking, for several seconds before he answered. "I don't take antidepressants," he answered, his voice totally void of expression. "Neither do I take pain medications of any sort, or anything else that might be addictive. I take vitamins, an assortment of essential minerals, and an occasional antacid before a race. I don't consume alcohol, don't use tobacco, don't eat fried foods. Anything else you'd like to know, *Doctor*?"

He was so defiant, so angry. Perhaps he'd have been better off going somewhere else, somewhere without the obvious emotional friction she seemed to be causing. That was her concern as a doctor coming out, of course, and not her personal need to be rid of him. "You don't have to stay here, and maybe it would be better if you didn't. I'll be glad to make arrangements to have you taken to another facility. There's an excellent clinic in Frankfurt, which isn't so far away, and we have a reciprocal arrangement with them."

"And I could have gone there, had I not chosen Aeberhard. But I wanted Aeberhard initially, and I'll stay here."

"Exactly why did you choose Aeberhard, Dante?" Catherine asked.

"You think it's because of you?"

"It's an odd coincidence so, yes, that did cross my mind."

He shook his head. "Reputation. That's all. You put skiers back into shape all the time. Do a nice job of it, actually. My injury is like what a skier might sustain. Also, this is closer to my home than any of the other places, so it made perfect sense for me to come here. *At the time*!"

Meaning that now, *at this time*, it didn't. Well, he was right about that. It didn't make sense to her, either. But what made even less sense was his insistence on staying. Too much water had flowed under the bridge for this to be anything but uncomfortable.

Catherine turned her focus to the castle in the distance, rather than staring back at Dante. His scrutiny made her nervous. It was like he was trying to read something in her, trying to probe deeper than he had a right to. Breaking the contact of his stare might make that jittery feeling skittering through her right now stop. "Just so you know, your X-rays are fine. Nothing out of the ordinary, which is why I called your previous doctor, to see what was going on. He told me you haven't been the model patient in the past two clinics you've been in. You checked out early, went home, injured yourself again. *Both times.* They didn't want you back. *Both times.*"

A slight smile cracked his face, a smile barely noticeable on his lips but quite apparent in his eyes. If she'd been looking. Which she was not. "And I didn't want to go back. Both times. Simple as that."

"With you it's never as simple as that. You always had an agenda, Dante. I can't imagine that has changed. In fact, I'm curious about your agenda in demanding that I be your physician. My guess is you mean to harass me because Friedrich Rilke is brilliant, and anybody with an ankle injury should want him rather than me, as that's his specialty. Then there's Dr Aeberhard, the best in the world. Yet you insist on me, which sounds like an agenda, as your *choice* goes against common sense."

"My *choice* sounds like a patient exerting a measure of control over his treatment. I always advocated that, Catherine. Always insisted that the doctor be a partner to the patient, not a medical dictator. That's the way the best medicine should work."

She twisted to look at him and noticed that his eyes sparked for a moment. It had happened before, when he'd mentioned medicine. Did Dante miss it? "You're suggesting that we be partners. But shouldn't partners get along?"

"I recall a time when we did." His tone lost its sharp edge for a instant. "And don't dismiss your abilities. You're good. I trust you to do what's best in my medical care."

"Oh, I don't dismiss my abilities, Dante. But you'd still be better off with Friedrich. If my ankle needed mending, he's the only one I'd go to." Catherine's voice was stiff. Dante couldn't help but hear the discomfort there because she could hear it herself.

"I'd be better off with the partner I choose, and I choose you. Like I said before, it's as simple as that."

"And like I said before, nothing's that simple with you, Dante." Their gazes drifted together for a moment, stayed fixed for a short time before both of them glanced away.

"Why the resort atmosphere, Catherine? And why would you choose to practice this kind of medicine? You were always so traditional."

"Dr Aeberhard, the founder of the clinic, believes that true healing has as much to do with non-medical issues as it does medical ones. He believes that a comfortable resort atmosphere is better suited to rehabilitation medicine than a hospital atmosphere would be."

"Do you?"

She finally turned to face him fully, surprised that all the edge and anger was gone from his voice. His scowl had vanished too, and the man sitting there, looking at her, was…Dante. Simply Dante, being interested in medicine the way he'd once been. "Actually, yes, I do. Back in Boston, when we…when I was doing my residency, then later, when I took my first real position, it was in a typical rehab hospital facility. Looked like a hospital, smelt like a hospital, functioned like a hospital, with all the regular hospital accouterments. We had good results, but there didn't seem to be anything spectacular happening. People came in broken, went out fixed. You know, typical course of treatment. When I arrived here, at Aeberhard, it was very different. People were happy. They recovered more quickly. In my opinion, a good many of the recoveries seemed more complete, and I knew there had to be a correlation between Dr Aeberhard's philosophies and the results I was seeing. It was exciting, Dante. This was a whole new medical concept for me, and I fell in love with it."

"You look happy," he said, actually sounding pleased about it.

"I am. It's a perfect situation for me." Had Dante found his perfect situation in auto racing? Judging from the way he acted, from all the stress she saw on his face and strain she heard in his voice, it didn't seem so. Of course, there might be other issues pressing on him...such as his child. Or a woman...a wife. "Look, Dante, your healing seems to be right on course. And you're lucky, considering that you've reinjured yourself since the initial injury and surgery. So the problem is just the healing process, which you seem to undermine."

He shifted his gaze off her to the outside. And straightened his shoulders. "Unfortunate accident."

"Remember, I talked to your other doctor," she said, her voice gentle. "I do know what happened. You went home too early, did too many things he'd told you not to do. It's not easy being laid up the way you are, and I understand that. But you can't keep going against medical advice."

"Just one person's opinion."

"Two, actually. Two very good surgeons—the original one who repaired you and the one who repaired you after you reinjured yourself. Both dismissed you as a patient when you went against their orders." A symptom of his fast lifestyle? Fast cars, fast women? Did he think he was impervious to the inevitable repercussions?

Her father had thought that, and it had gotten him killed.

"It was taking too long. I should have been up and about much sooner. They weren't pushing me hard enough, and I don't have months and months to spend on recovery. I need it...faster."

"Is that a medical diagnosis?" she asked. "Because, as I recall, you were a general surgeon, not an orthopedic or rehabilitation specialist."

"You know what they say…that doctors make the worst patients."

"Except you're a race-car driver who's on the verge of losing a career if he doesn't follow his doctor's orders. It's just that critical now. If you injure yourself again, there's no guarantee you'll ever walk normally, Dante. More than that, you might lose your ability to drive competitively. And while I'm not going so far as to say these were self-inflicted injuries, they were caused because you didn't listen. Or you thought you knew more than your doctors did."

"They wanted me flat in bed, or in a wheelchair, for a ridiculous amount of time. I don't have time for that."

"So let me guess. You got up, went home, resumed normal activities immediately…"

"An entire week after surgery. They replace hips and send patients home, *walking*, in three days."

"And a shattered ankle repair is far more complicated than a total hip replacement." Catherine sighed impatiently. "You're the patient here, Dante. Not the doctor. You're going to have to act like a patient if you expect us to do our best work."

"I thought I was the guest."

In spite of herself, Catherine laughed. "Were you always this contentious?"

He chuckled, then smiled. "That was one of the things that attracted you to me. You even said so on a few occasions. I believe you said you liked your men with some backbone."

"Well, if I did, then I was blinded by…other things." She bit back a smile of her own. "Because it's not a very attractive feature on you now." That was a lie, actually. Before, she'd never argued back with him. But now she liked the little tingle that arguing with Dante caused. Although he didn't need to know that.

"Or you're not admitting it. You do have the side of you that tends to hold things back, or see them the way you think they should be. I'm willing to bet that hasn't changed."

That little bit of lightness that had crept into her mood suddenly sobered, good and hard. This was getting too close now, too personal, too uncomfortable. Well, she wouldn't have it. Absolutely would not have it! "What hasn't changed is that I'm the doctor, you're the patient, and I want to give you the best medical treatment I know how to give. And to be honest, Dante, I'm concerned about your medical progress. You're not co-operative and you're not a good patient." Nice, safe ground. She felt better here. "Put all that together and I'm worried that in another few days you'll up and do what you've done before, go against medical advice and injure yourself again. You're only six days post-operative right now. The hospital in Italy sent you out here as fast as they could because of your checkered history, according to the director of orthopedics. He said he hoped we would have better luck with you and, frankly, I'm worried about that. So, you were a bright doctor. What would you suggest? What would you do if you were the doctor treating a stubborn, rebellious patient such as yourself?"

"You know, I meant to ask you…how did you come to be director here? You don't have that many years in the field. Seems to me Dr Aeberhard, with his reputation, might have gone after someone with more experience. And you, if I'm correct, would have had only three or four years in actual practice after your residency, which doesn't seem like much when it comes to taking over admin duties at a clinic such as this."

"Medical admin only," she corrected. The day-to-day activities of the patient care they offered. "Max still manages the business aspects. And rather than getting involved in an argument over whether or not I have the proper qualifications for my position, which is what you were trying to start, probably as a way to shift attention off the fact that you're a very bad patient and don't want to talk about it, let's get back to what I was talking about. Your attitude. And here's what I've decided. You'll follow orders—all medical orders—for as long as you're here."

"That's it?"

"What were you expecting? Sedatives and restraints to tie you to the bed? We don't do that here, Dante. What we do is treat patients who want to be treated. If we see that they don't, we have a long waiting list and not nearly enough beds to accommodate that, so we ask them to leave. So if you want to recover, you'll follow the protocol we outline for you. And if you don't, we'll hire a limousine service that will take you into Bern. From there…well, in truth, I don't care what you do or where you go." Catherine stood. "Now, I have an appointment with another patient. You're welcome to stay here and relax, return to your suite, go to the spa…whatever you'd like to do. Today is free for you. Therapy will start tomorrow." With that, she started to walk away.

Halfway to the entrance, Dante caught up to her, wheeling alongside her. "I need to be in form to race by spring," he said.

"Then you have a long way to go."

"I looked for you, Catherine."

That stopped her on the spot, and she spun around to face him. He'd actually looked for her? "When?" she asked, trying not to sound too giddy.

"Shortly after my first surgery."

A tiny jolt of disappointment surged through her. She wasn't sure what she'd expected to hear—that he'd searched shortly after they'd called it quits, or maybe some time quite a while later, when he'd come to his senses and realized what he'd left behind. Perhaps those were words she would have liked hearing, but what she had heard made better sense, especially coming from someone like Dante. He'd looked for her *only* after he'd needed her medical expertise. Not because he'd needed her. "You thought that I might have something to say about the kind of therapy you'd need? Is that why you tried to find me?" Even though she knew the truth, she still wanted to hear something else, silly as that seemed.

"Something like that. I always respected your opinion. You were a good doctor, and I wanted to see what you might recommend…"

Well, there it was. The true pronouncement that their past was merely an insignificant blip in Dante's life, just as she'd suspected. Nothing that mattered to him. He couldn't have made that more clear. Catherine bent down to his wheelchair, placed her hands flat on the armrests and stared him straight in the eyes. "You may have respected my opinion, Dante, but you never respected me."

"When did this happen to you, Catherine?" he asked, his dark eyes suddenly gleaming. What was that in them? Mischief?

"When did what happen?"

"This need to challenge every little detail." He patted the armrests on his wheelchair. "If I called these armrests, you'd call them something else, then put it in the medical chart that way to make it so." He paused, studied her expression for a moment—an expression she was fighting to hold blank—then continued. "It's attractive on you, actually. And to be honest, I don't know if that's the way you were when we were together and I simply didn't notice, or if it's something new. Either way, it's a good attitude for you. Sexy as hell."

She sucked in a sharp breath and straightened up. This banter was blatantly sexual between them, and wrong. She knew where it could lead, what it could do. And it was so damn easy to fall victim to the Dante effect, which was where she was headed *again*, if she wasn't careful. "You're good, Dante. I'll give you credit where it's due."

"Good? At what?"

He arched his eyebrows, trying to feign innocence, but Catherine knew that expression. Knew it because she'd fallen for it so many times. "Is this how you do it? How you charm your women into bed?" *How he'd charmed her into bed so soon, so easily, after their first meeting?*

"Is it working?"

Catherine shook her head as she felt her resistance trickling away. Time to regain control. Time to fight off the Dante effect. "Maybe you being here is a coincidence, Dante. I don't think you'd lie to me about that. But you're not going to make light of what we do here, and you're not going to sabotage your recovery and charm your way out of it. I don't have time for that, and don't have time for you if that's how you're going to behave." So now the test of wills was on, and Dante thought he would win. Well, not if she had anything to do with it. "And while we're on the subject, I don't like the fact that you're trying to go against my authority. You may not respect me as a person, and that's fine, but you owe me professional respect, and if you can't agree to that, you'll have your dismissal papers within the hour. Ultimately, I can make that decision."

"It's a pity…" he replied, then didn't finish the sentence. Rather, he spun around and wheeled out the solarium door, leaving her dangling, waiting to find out what, exactly, the pity was.

Catherine waited until he was halfway down the way into the hall before she took the bait, chased after him, then asked, "What's a pity?"

"That your marriage hasn't mellowed you more."

"I'm not married," she said, totally unaffected. "Not any more."

Dante arched his eyebrows, the odd expression on his face a precursor to something she wasn't sure she wanted to hear him say. But instead of replying, retorting or otherwise offering some kind of sarcastic remark, which was what she expected from him, Dante merely wheeled away, leaving her stunned by his lack of response.

* * *

"Damn," he muttered, slamming shut the door to his suite. The game had been fun when she'd been off limits. Admittedly, he'd felt a little twinge of jealousy when he'd learned she was Mrs Wilder, and not Miss Brannon. But that was for old time's sake, he supposed. And he'd been enjoying this little game of flirtation he'd been putting on. It had been safe. Something to pass the time, to keep his mind sharp while he was here. He'd enjoyed it, and if he'd been reading Catherine correctly, he thought she did, too.

But damn it all! He was flirting with someone who was *not* a married woman, and that's when it got dangerous. His life didn't accommodate relationships. Just flings. And precious few of those nowadays. Somehow, running off to spend the night with a willing beauty didn't have the punch to it that it used to, before Gianni came into his life. Actually, before Catherine, too.

Lately, the more satisfying punch for him was the emotional one. He was a happy, contented man, for the most part. He didn't need those empty nights with faces he couldn't remember the next morning. In fact, Catherine had been someone he'd thought would fall into that category when he'd met her...another in the line. A pretty colleague who attracted him, but only for a little while. Except he hadn't been able to move on, and he'd caught himself liking that. Then had come his responsibilities to Gianni, and it had all blurred together—his old life, his reputation, the new aspects of his life that pretty well consumed almost everything of him.

Hell, he couldn't even remember the last time he'd been with a woman, that's how long it had been. The racing sensation, Dante Baldassare, a real ladies' man, truly was not. In reality, he was much less than his reputation made him out to be. But he did have his *inflated*, if not fictitious, image to mind, after all. It was part of the façade his sister Gina, as the Baldassare publicist, demanded of him. Part of the racing package. A huge part of what made the Baldassare racing team successful, and admired worldwide.

Just not part of *him*.

So, it should have been an innocent flirt with Catherine. But divorced as she was, she'd probably been dragged over the emotional rocks enough. As much as she'd hurt him when she'd left him, he wasn't vindictive enough to want her hurt back. Harass maybe, as she suspected. But never hurt.

But she did slap back at him with rather a salty punch, didn't she? Like she'd never done before. So, what was that about?

Dante thought about it for a moment, then transferred himself into bed and decided to call Gianni. It really didn't matter what it was about with Catherine, he decided as he picked up the phone. She was now in the off-limits column. And that was a real pity, because she might have made these next dreary weeks a little more fun.

CHAPTER FOUR

IT WAS going on midnight when Catherine finally decided to call it quits for the day. Her feet ached, she was exhausted, both physically and mentally, and a dull headache was beginning around her temples. Along with all the turmoil surrounding Dante, which turned into her returning about two hours of phone calls to various reporters, she'd seen fifteen other patients today, chaired a board meeting and met with a pharmaceutical representative.

Now, her eighteen hours for the day were done, and it was time to go home and crawl into bed. Good thing home was on the other side of the compound—a nice little chalet within a three-minute walk of the clinic building. There were times when she thought she should move farther away if, for no other reason than to give herself more separation between her personal life and her job. But who was she kidding? She didn't have a personal life, and if not for her job, she'd have no life at all. Besides, on nights like this, when she could barely drag one foot in front of the other, her cozy little bed being three minutes away did have an appeal.

On her way out, Catherine impulsively detoured to the hall where Dante's suite was located. It was a nice suite—a large living room, a spacious bedroom with all the amenities of the finest hotel, a second, smaller bedroom for a guest, a modest waiting room just inside the entry, and a tiny area with kitchen facilities. Not to mention a lavish bathroom she'd die to have for herself.

As Catherine grew closer to Dante's suite, she had a quick rethink on coming in this direction. It was silly. There was nothing to see. Nothing to do here. Nothing to argue, either. Yet the unexplained draw tugged her along the hallway until she was practically standing at his door.

"Dr Wilder," Nurse Reasnor said, as she passed by Catherine, scurrying her way to deliver a shot of insulin to Mr Aylesworth. "Is there something I can do for you?" she asked, the speculative arching of her eyebrows making it quite clear she wasn't used to seeing Catherine, or any one else here, at this time of the night.

"Just taking the long way out on my way home," she said. "Thought I'd see how my patient was doing."

"Mr Baldassare? He's doing fine. I looked in on him about an hour ago, took his vital signs, checked his ankle, and everything seemed to be in order."

Catherine acknowledged her response with a polite smile, and moved past Dante's door, padding along the marble floor, telling herself how silly this little quest was. There was no need to be here. Dante was, most likely, long asleep, as were most of the guests. Wandering by his door had no point, especially as he'd already had his nightly medical check and she couldn't use that for an excuse.

At the end of the hall, she stopped by the nursing station for a moment, made a pretense of studying a patient chart—one other than Dante's—even though she really didn't need an excuse to be there, but having one made her feel less silly. After that she finally headed back the way she'd come, only to be stopped by Dante, who opened his door at the exact same time she walked by it.

"I thought I heard your voice," he said, his voice in a whisper. "Do you live here or do you ever go home?"

"Actually, I suppose you could say that I do live here." She did feel a little awkward at being caught. "Why are you up so late?" The doctor in her kicked in. "Are you in pain? Should I prescribe something?"

"Couldn't sleep. Wanted to make myself a cup of tea, and the teas stocked in my pantry are all herbal. I was going to see if I could find regular, black tea."

"With caffeine? Are you sure that's what you want at this time of the night?"

"Do you ever go off duty, Catherine? Just unwind for a little while and quit being a doctor concerned with everybody's well-being?"

She laughed. "It doesn't seem that way, does it?" The truth was, she never did. Even when she was at home, she was on call for consultations, emergency treatment or whatever was needed. "Look, you go back into your suite, and I'll see what I can find for you."

"Will you join me for a cup?" he asked.

She hesitated, at first inclined to refuse. That would have been the easiest, most sensible thing to do, but her resolve faltered. What could a little civility between them hurt after all? It could be nice, as a matter of fact. Something to put her patient at ease. At least, that's what she was telling herself this was about as she caught herself nodding. "I think I will."

"You're welcome to the herbal," he said.

Catherine wrinkled her nose. "I may advocate it, like a good doctor should, but that doesn't mean I like it."

Five minutes later, Catherine returned with tea and a tin of biscuits she'd scrounged from the kitchen. Since she had to be back on duty in less than six hours now, this wasn't what she needed to be doing. She knew that, and on her way to the kitchen she'd convinced herself to drop the tea and biscuits off at Dante's suite and hurry along home. But on her way back from the kitchen she'd argued herself out of that decision once more by assuring herself that a few minutes wouldn't hurt. Now, at his door, she was vacillating, on the verge of going back to her first decision to go straight home.

Then Dante opened the door, and the dim light from the hall caught his face in silhouette, causing a barely perceptible gasp to escape her lips. So handsome…Suddenly, the years between them disappeared, and this was Catherine standing at the door to Dante's apartment in Boston, waiting to enter, waiting to tumble into the arms and into the bed of the man she'd known, even then, could break her heart. She hadn't cared back then, and at this moment, with her next work day separated from this moment by only the thinnest ribbon of sleep, she didn't care now. She entered, and shut the door behind her.

"I'm surprised you came back," he said, wheeling his way to the small kitchen. "I didn't expect you to. I figured you'd have second thoughts and drop off the tea with Nurse Reasnor so she could deliver it." He already had the kettle on, the steam from it on the verge of rolling into a whistle.

"I didn't expect me to either," she said, placing teabags into the two cups he'd set out. "But since I'd lost half a night's sleep already, I didn't figure another few minutes would make much of a difference one way or another. And tea sounded good." Almost as good as a little quiet time with Dante.

"You keep horrible hours, Catherine," Dante commented, handing her a plate for the biscuits. "That's probably the thing about being a doctor I miss least—the ungodly hours. In racing, we can keep horrible hours if we want, but it's a choice, not a requirement like it is in medicine, where it's simply part of the job."

"I can deal with it. I've been doing it for years, and I'm used to it."

"Used to it, maybe, but it's not good for you on a regular basis, and those bags under your eyes tell me it's on a regular basis. Besides, so many hours of work, and no play, will make you very old, very fast. And you don't ever play, do you, Catherine? Somehow I imagine that you don't."

He was correct. She didn't. But she didn't answer him. No need to seem so pathetic or desperate. Rather, she placed the biscuits on the plate, handed it back to Dante, and carried the cups of tea over to the table in the bayed alcove, with windows that looked out over the expanse of the foothills just beyond Aeberhard. At this time of the night, the white sea of newly fallen snow was awash with twinkling lights from cottages and chalets dotting the countryside, more in isolated glimmers standing well apart from each other than in tight clumps like fairy-lights on a Christmas tree. That was one of the things she loved most about this area—people didn't feel the need to cram themselves together. They stretched out, appreciating the countryside and surrounding themselves with it. Yet they were neighbors, even if they did nestle in separately at what might have been several city blocks by American standards. Breathing room—that's the way she thought of it. The people here allowed themselves breathing room.

"It's beautiful at night," she said, taking a seat at the table. "I'm not sure I could ever return to the United States, after seeing all this. Over there it's too…"

"Crowded," Dante supplied, wheeling himself in under the table. "That it is, and I hate crowds."

"But you attract crowds."

"In my professional life, yes. That's part of it. But I have other, more private parts of my life where the crowds and notoriety are not allowed. For instance, I live in a little area in Tuscany much like this—many neighbors, but not so close in." He smiled. "Plenty of breathing room there."

"When we were together I never knew you lived in Tuscany," she said. She'd known he was from Italy, but it had never occurred to her to ask where. And it had never occurred to him to tell her until after he'd left her

"In a lemon grove, actually. My villa sits up on a hill over-looking my few trees. It's a very small grove, and a small villa, but it suits me. And I have all the breathing room I need there."

She saw the wistfulness come over him as he talked of it. Surprising as it seemed, having had a torrid affair with this man, she'd never seen that expression before. "What do you do with the lemons?" she asked, not sure why she even cared.

"Give them away." He laughed. "You can only make so much lemonade, then you have to do something else with the lemons, so my friends and neighbors are allowed to come pick as they need."

"You're a farmer, then." Now, that was a surprise. Doctor, racer, farmer…a man of many talents.

"I suppose you could say that, couldn't you? But I do have to admit I don't tend the lemon grove so much as merely own it. It's more a hobby, I think."

"Do you miss medicine, Dante?"

That wistfulness returned. "At times. I was the one who strayed from the family fold to go into medicine, and I think that was more from rebellion than anything else. My family was very demanding. At least I thought so when I was young. It didn't seem like I was given any choices—I would race. It was expected, but I was the restless one who wanted to see what else the world had in store for me.

"Dario stayed with the family, carried on the racing tradition. It made my parents happy that one of us did as we were supposed to do. But I was the one who always had to do things differently, so I became a doctor. I'd always wanted it, my father didn't encourage it, which probably made me want it all the more." He shrugged as he picked up his teacup. "None of which matters now. I'm back in the family fold, doing what was expected of me all along, carrying on the tradition I was always meant to be part of. And I like it. I'm glad to be back because I've discovered that racing is as much a part of me as being a surgeon was.

Unfortunately, they are two different lives that can't fit together." He chuckled, but sadly. "Dario always told me I'd come back. He wanted me to so we could race against each other. Two Baldassares on the track at the same time, as teammates and competitors. I'm sorry I missed that opportunity, and caused my brother to miss it."

"I'm so sorry about your brother," she said. He'd told her the vague details of Dario's death, but had never elaborated. She'd read the rest in an old sports magazine. It had been a car crash during a race in France. He was said to have been the best driver during that particular race, and no one knew, for sure, what had happened, apart from a little slickness on the track. Just one of those fluke accidents—something she knew so well from her work, from her life. From her father. "It must have been very difficult for your family, losing him that way. And for you. Twins are so close…"

Dante nodded. "It was, and we were. But we're a close family, which helped us all get through it."

"And you took your brother's place?"

He shot her a caustic glance over his teacup. "Not *his* place. I took my own place in racing. The place I was supposed to be and too stubborn to admit that I wanted it."

And had done very well in it, from all accounts. "And your career as a surgeon?"

He shrugged. "I tell myself I'll go back to it someday, and maybe I will. But I don't know. Life gets complicated, and I'm not sure it's wise to make too many plans. Lesson learned the hard way."

"But you would?" She sensed real sadness in him. Maybe he was a man torn between the love of too many lives. Her father had been, and in the end it had hurt him deeply. Had hurt her so deeply, too.

"Perhaps." He picked up a biscuit, studied it for a moment, then gave it a lackluster toss back onto the plate. "But right now I'm a racer. That's all there is. The car, the race course and a damned broken ankle keeping me from being where I need to be."

"Does anybody else in your family race?" His family name was big in the sport, but that's all she knew.

"My father and his brother own the racing team. Cristofor works on the mechanic crew. He's been behind the wheel a few times, but we'll wait and see what catches on for him and if he decides he wants to drive later on. And I have two cousins, one who's starting to come along in racing and one who intends to drive when he's a little older. He's only fifteen now. Also, my mother manages the business aspects, and two of my three sisters arrange all the publicity and handle the events we're required to attend." He smiled, raised the cup to his lips. "Then I have several nephews, all who want to race. But that's a decision a long way into the future as none of them is over the age of eight. Instead of slapping the baby's behind when a Baldassare child is born, it's said the doctor gives them a pair of racing goggles and a helmet." He chuckled, then took a sip of his tea.

This was nice, and as she sipped her own tea she actually relaxed, slid down a little in her seat and felt all the tension drain right out of her. Dante had always had that effect on her, something as good as a massage. At the end of a rotten day, even if whatever happened between them wouldn't lead to the bedroom, just being with him relaxed her in ways nothing else ever had.

"Better than a sedative," she said, not meaning for that to slip out.

"Excuse me?"

Time to leave before she relaxed enough to say something she would regret. Catherine pushed her cup aside, and stood. "Since I've got to go back to work in a few hours, I think I need to at least appear like I've slept. But this has been nice, Dante. Very surprising, very pleasant. And nice." She sincerely meant that.

"And tomorrow you'll turn back into that mean, rather dictatorial doctor, won't you? It's a pity, Catherine. I like you better this way." He followed her to the door. "The question is, which way do you like yourself?"

She should take offense, as this was none of his business. Nothing about her was his business. But she was too tired, and she didn't want to give up the lingering mellow feeling that was fighting to hang on. So she decided to let it go. No fight left in her tonight. "The way I like me is the way I function best for my patients." She laid her hand on the doorknob. "That's all there is, Dante. All there can be for me. All I want."

"You always wanted so much more, Catherine." He rolled up alongside her and laid his hand on top of hers. "There's always so more to be had if you want it, and I can't believe that you don't."

The spark that arced between them felt more like a flame, and she jerked her hand out from under his. Before, they'd had sparks, but not like this. She looked at the back of her hand for a moment, nearly expecting to see the tracing of a slight burn. When she didn't, she grabbed the doorknob fast and opened the door, then quickly stepped into the hall before something like that happened again. Then she turned back to face Dante. "Maybe there's more to be had, but I don't want it, Dante. None of it. What I have now is exactly what I'd planned for my life and I don't want that to change." With that, she turned and hurried away.

The exit loomed in the distance, and she was still hurrying to get out of there, to get home to claim sleep in the few hours left to her, when the page came in. In the form of her cellphone jingle, though. "We have an anaphylactic reaction in Room 118," the voice on the other end told her. "Dr Meijer is with another patient who's having chest pains, so as you're on call…"

So much for sleep. Catherine spun round and ran in the opposite direction, her feet slapping hard on the floor. She turned at the first corner, barely clearing the wall in her haste, and dashed straight into Room 118, where Mrs Gunter, a middle-aged, strikingly beautiful woman recovering from a bad fall and a shattered knee, was having trouble getting her breath. She was wheezing, panicking, her color was going dusky and Nurse Muller wasn't being too successful at quieting the woman down.

For good reason. When Catherine took a look, the first thing she noticed was that the woman's airway was significantly swollen. She was slowly suffocating. "I want Benedryl in the IV, stat," she called. Benedryl had strong properties to combat allergic reactions. "And get me an oxygen set-up."

Catherine took another look, saw that the woman's lips were going blue now. Putting a stethoscope to her chest, what she heard made her realize that she had to get an airway established immediately or Mrs Gunter was going to die. What little air going in and out was barely enough to sustain life, and with each passing second that capacity was decreasing. This woman wasn't going to survive if Catherine didn't get her breathing established, right now! Benedryl wasn't going to be fast enough, damn it! "I want Dr Meijer in here!" she shouted. "Get him!"

"Can't!" Nurse Muller cried, running out the door after the emergency supplies. "His patient is—

"Then get me a tracheotomy set-up. And find another nurse to help me prep my patient for surgery. Now!"

No time to waste, no time to ponder anything other than what she had to do. Catherine cranked the head of the bed flat, pulled out the pillows and shoved away the bedside stand and chair to give herself better access. Then she returned to her patient to have another listen to her chest. Breath sounds were diminishing more, and Mrs Gunter was beginning to lose consciousness. Her life expectancy was now reduced to minutes, and precious few of those. "We're going to get you breathing right away," Catherine reassured, even though the woman's eyes were closed and she was close to going unconscious.

She didn't want to perform a tracheotomy—that was a job for a surgeon, and one she'd done only as a student, and then only a couple of times. But there wasn't another choice here. She had to do it, and as she was prepping herself, her mind clicking through the process in rapid bullet points, Nurse Muller flew back into the room, followed by Nurse Reasnor, who'd been on duty in Dante's wing. One nurse carried the surgical kit, the other carried the drugs Catherine had ordered.

Without a word, Catherine grabbed the kit, tore it open, and found the Betadine scrub. But as she was about to open it, Dante appeared at the bedside. "I can do this," he said. "If you want me to."

No argument, no time to question him. She knew he could. It was in his eyes, that old look she used to love when he was about to go into surgery. The determination that he was about to do something he loved, something good. In the best interests of what Mrs Gunter needed, it was a surgeon, and without a word Catherine stepped aside.

After Dante had pulled on a pair of surgical gloves, she poured disinfectant over Mrs Gunter's neck and in the blink of an eye he sliced an incision across the woman's neck, inserted his fingers into the wound through to her windpipe and pulled back enough tissue so that Mrs Gunter was able to draw in a good breath, one that sailed past all the swelling that had tried to stop it.

At the same time Catherine took the plastic tracheotomy tube from the kit and slipped it into Mrs Gunter's neck. It would keep her air passage open and allow her to breathe through it until the swelling was gone. A minute later it was in place, oxygen was running into it, and medications were flowing into the patient's veins.

Crisis averted in mere minutes. Mrs Gunter was going to be fine in another few hours, amazing as that seemed. "Thank you," she said. "I'm not sure I'd have been fast enough to…I haven't done a trach in years, and…" She gave him a genuine smile. "I'm glad you came along when you did."

"I wasn't sure you'd let me. It was a simple procedure, but after all this time—"

"You were good," she interrupted, as another thought washed over her now that the emergency was over. "You always were. But, tell me, how did you know what was happening?"

"Natural reaction. Nurse Reasnor was in my room, trying to convince me to take a sleeping pill, when she got the call. I heard there wasn't a surgeon on duty, and I didn't even think about it." He shrugged. "I just came."

Was that it, really? "Did you think I wasn't capable?" she snapped. "Is that it? You didn't think I could do what needed to be done? I mean, you did question me being director here, so were you also questioning my ability to perform a tracheotomy? Is that what this was about, Dante?"

He opened his mouth to respond, then thought better of it and backed away. "Goodnight, Catherine." Stiff voice, stiff demeanor. Angry face. "I hope you get some sleep tonight." With that, Dante spun around and wheeled away, leaving Catherine to watch after him until he disappeared around the corner. She was numb. Numb and totally dumbstruck because she wasn't sure. Had him taking over been a natural reaction, as he'd said, or a decision based on something else, such as his doubting her abilities?

She wanted to believe it had been an innocent, decent gesture. Truly wanted to believe that. But her life history was fraught with so many people stepping in, taking control, making decisions for her without first asking her, that she truly didn't know. And right now she didn't have time to figure it out as she needed to take another look at Mrs Gunter. But even as she assessed the woman's breathing, which had returned to normal, and took her vital signs, which were evening out, she wondered about Dante's motives. *For the patient*, she told herself. *He did what he did for the patient*. Thinking anything else was silly, and a bit self-centered. Dante was a good doctor—*still a good doctor*—and it shone through. He might have a love of racing, but his love of medicine was still there, too. And that's what it had been about. Nothing else. Absolutely nothing else.

She was glad he'd been the one to do the procedure, and the way she'd turned on him hadn't been fair. Wasn't totally unexpected either, given their personal situation. Even so, she owed Dante an apology.

Why am I being so reactionary?

Because she was letting her personal life slip over into her professional life. Something she never did. *Time to get a grip, Catherine.* Time to get a great big grip and put a wall up between the two.

But an hour later, as she sat across from Mrs Gunter's bed, still trying to chart the notes about the incident, she simply couldn't get that wall to go into place. Not when all she could think about was Dante.

And it was neither Dante the doctor nor Dante the racer whose image just wouldn't go away. It was Dante the man she'd loved.

He hated the bed, ultra-plush as it was. Hated the room. Hated every damned thing about this place. Most of all he hated it that he wasn't able to get up and pace the floor. He liked to pace. It worked off the frustration, gave him some exercise doing it, allowed him to think on his feet. Somehow, rolling back and forth on the cold, tile floor in his wheelchair didn't have the same cathartic effect, and tonight he needed that effect. Desperately. Too many things bottled up in him, with no escape valve.

Dante glanced at the clock. Much too late to call Gianni now. He wanted to, even though he'd talked to him earlier—twice, actually. The second time Rosa had scolded him about worrying so much. She was taking good care of Gianni, she said, and after raising six children she knew how to do it just fine, thank you very much! She was right, but that still didn't ease his mounting frustration. He missed his son.

Of course, when he mentioned that to his mother, the discussion—or actually, admonition—turned into the same old thing he'd heard dozens of times. Gianni needed more stability in his life. "A child deserves a home and family, Dante. We gave that to you and you owe it to Gianni. He's already had so much turmoil…"

Oh, Dante knew the argument. He'd heard it every time he'd bundled Gianni up to take with him on the racing circuit. They wanted stability for their grandson, which to them meant a mother to stay home and care for him. Except Dante wasn't in a marrying mood, and certainly recruiting a wife for the sole purpose of being Gianni's mother was out of the question. So was leaving Gianni with any number of family members. Ruling out all the unacceptable options, Dante was doing the best he could as a father. And he took the responsibility seriously.

But it wasn't a traditional lifestyle, at least not by his parents' standards. That's just how he and Gianni lived, though. Well, the two of them plus Gianni's nanny and his tutor. They traveled along during race season, and when the season was over life turned more normal for everyone concerned. Dante and Gianni lived back in Tuscany as a regular family, then. They had daily routines, Gianni went to a regular school. They picked lemons. But during the race season…well, as far as Dante was concerned, there wasn't another choice to be made. Gianni was with him on the road in spite of all the objections. And to prove that he was right about that, Gianni was a normal, happy, healthy little boy who was well advanced in his schooling. Not having a regular roof over his head every night for half the year wasn't hurting him.

Although Dante did foresee a time in the future when Gianni might want to settle down more, make steady friends, go to a regular school for the full year. But that was some way off. Too far ahead to think about now. And right now…all he had to think about was this damnable place.

And Catherine!

Admittedly, a good part of this bad mood was about what had just happened—the way Catherine had accused him of practically forcing her into the position of being controlled. That wasn't the case. He'd just meant to help, yet she'd taken a simple act and twisted it into something it hadn't been. And that just plain stung.

Oh, sure. He'd made a horrendous mistake all those years ago by not including her in his plans and, in essence, just expecting her to go along with whatever he'd wanted. He'd paid for that, though, in more ways than one. More than that, he regretted what he'd done because that had cost him the only woman he'd ever seen a future with. But live and learn. At least, he hoped he'd learned his lesson. Catherine didn't think so, apparently. That much was obvious in the way she'd twisted a simple gesture into something ugly, with ulterior motives.

What was also obvious was that she'd certainly moved on with her life. Done a respectable job of it. He was proud of her, even if what she'd chosen for herself was so narrow. "Get over it," he muttered, as he finally wheeled up to his bed. "It's all in the past." Except that telling himself to get over it and getting over it were two different things, and after an hour of tossing and turning and staring up at the dark ceiling, he finally consented to a mild sedative from Nurse Reasnor. Even after he'd taken it, he went through another twenty minutes of fretting before he finally drifted off into a fitful sleep. As he did so, the last thought that danced through his mind was of Catherine.

CHAPTER FIVE

"How's he doing this morning?" Catherine asked. She hadn't gone into the room with the whirlpool yet. Rather, she was standing in the doorway, watching Dante take his morning therapy. He was immersed in the tub, sitting in soothing water midway up his chest, gently working out the kinks in his ankle by moving it in small, slow circles as Hans, the physical therapist, watched. It was a quiet, almost somber scene, with Dante scowling at nothing in particular and Hans casting Catherine speculative glances.

"Not very talkative, but he's co-operating," Hans confided in a low voice. "He has a lot of stiffness to work out before we can even begin to see what he has left in the way of strength, yet the first thing he asked me when they brought him down was when he would be up and about on his own. The man clearly doesn't want to be here and I'm worried that he'll quit in the middle of what I have planned for him and leave Aeberhard."

"Which is what got him in trouble before. Dante's impatient. And demanding of himself. Very bad patient."

"Do you think he'll go against orders?" Hans asked.

"I hope not but, to be honest, I don't know. He's got a lot more at stake this time because his career is on the line, and I have to hope he's finally coming to terms with his limitations and what it's going to take for him to work through them." She nodded an acknowledgment as Dante finally looked in her direction, but he did not respond to her in any way. Perhaps today was a good day to take herself off his case no matter what he wanted as she was clearly not the doctor best suited to his needs. Not to mention the undertow of all their personal issues pulling them both down. "But he's smart. He knows what he has to do, even if he doesn't want to do it. So I'm hoping he'll listen to reason, because if he doesn't…" She finished off her sentence with a shrug.

"Well, I've seen him race," Hans admitted. "In person, as often as I can. He's good and I hope we can get him rehabilitated because watching him race is worth the price of a ticket."

Another fan. It was still hard to believe that Dante had fans…fans who were people she knew, people she respected. In her mind, in the image of him that wouldn't go away, he still wore surgical scrubs, and his only fans were the patients whose lives he saved. "What, exactly, constitutes 'good' about his driving?" To be honest, she'd never watched a race. Couldn't find the heart to do it.

"He pushes the speed more than some of the other drivers, takes the curves a little tighter, risks a pass where no one else will. That builds up the overall sport, makes it thrilling for the spectator. In other words, being good means taking more risks. Coming closer to death."

Life came with enough risks without adding to them on purpose. She knew that intellectually, as well as emotionally, knew the awful results it could bring, not only on the ones taking the risks but on the people who loved them. *Especially on the people who loved them.* She'd never seen that daredevil streak in Dante when they'd been together. Never suspected it might exist in him or else she wouldn't have even given him that first tumble. But it was there, wasn't it? Which made her glad their affair had been nothing more than that—an affair. *Without risk.*

Unless the twinges of her heart that she'd refused to call a broken heart could be considered a risk.

"After he's through here, go ahead and fit him to a walker, will you?" Catherine asked. "It's time to see what he can do on his feet."

"He's not going to like that. Somehow I'll bet he's more the type for a cane, ego and all considered."

Catherine laughed. "He is that type, isn't he? But I still want him to start out on a walker. It's safer."

"He'll refuse," Hans warned.

"No, he won't." She sounded confident, but truth was, she wasn't. Dante could, and probably would, refuse. "If he wants to get back into that race car come next season, and if he fully intends to do more than sit in it, he'll co-operate. Remind him of that when he gets stubborn. Tell him if he refuses the prescribed therapy, I won't certify his health and he'll never get back to racing." Which, actually, might be a blessing. But that was only a personal opinion that had no place here.

Catherine assessed two more patients under her care as they went about their morning therapy routines, then returned to her office, only to meet up with Max, who was simply staring out the window as he waited for her.

"Mrs Gunter has a peanut allergy," he said. "She ate candy with peanuts in it, and that's what caused her allergic reaction last night. She knows better, but she thought one little taste wouldn't hurt her."

"It almost killed her," Catherine said, sitting down behind her desk. "I'll stop by later this morning and have a little chat with her—let her know how close she came to dying." For some people that worked. For some, it didn't—like Dante, and her father.

"I understand Mr Baldassare, or should I say Dr Baldassare, saved her life?"

"He is still a surgeon and, yes, he did." She thought about defending herself, and telling Max that she could have performed that procedure to the same end, but the truth was that Dante had been better at it. She knew that, and she wasn't about to downplay it. "I was glad he was there to do the trach. I'm rusty. Dante's skills were still perfect."

Max gave her a brisk nod of approval. "Glad you didn't let your personal feelings get in the way. Seeing how you react to this man…"

"I don't react to this man, Max. And you know my personal feelings never get in the way of patient care," she said defensively.

He chuckled. "You're reacting to him now."

She wanted to protest, tell him she wasn't, but that seemed childish. Especially when she did react to Dante. Maybe even overreacted. "I'm glad he was here to perform the procedure. If nothing else, Mrs Muller will have a much neater scar from his incision than she would have had from mine."

"Which brings me to another point. We're growing, Catherine. More patients wanting to come here, which means we're dealing with more physical ills than those we normally treat here. We're also getting considerably more enquiries now that Mr Baldassare is here. I've been thinking…"

Catherine drew in a sharp breath. Was he about to dismiss her? Growth was inevitable. Perhaps he wanted someone more qualified to take her place? She'd thought that when he'd first hired her, and the initial weeks of her employment were filled with enormous uncertainty. She'd eventually got over that, though. Now here it was, back again. One of the patients had done a better job than she could have possibly done on a simple surgical procedure, and she feared Max was having second thoughts about keeping her there.

He turned round to face her. "We need a larger medical staff, one with varied training. We treat broken bodies, but we need to be better able to take care of other emergencies and medical situations that arise. There should have been more than two doctors in the clinic last night. And I'm not downplaying your skills,

Catherine. You're a fine doctor and a very sound administrator. But you're not a surgeon and you should have never been forced into a position where you might have had to perform a procedure, even if it was minor."

"We've done well with our staffing the way it is," she replied. "There's always someone on call, ready to cover."

"Until last night. And we were damned lucky Baldassare was here. So I've been thinking that it's time to do better. I can't take call on the night shift any longer. I haven't done it for months now, and I think that limits us, which isn't good. And you're working far too many hours making up for my lack. That's not good either, Catherine. Not for you, and not for the patients you might put at risk when you're exhausted."

"I'll hire more staff," she said, not sure where this was going.

"That's a start, but I think the first thing you should do is dismiss me. I can't pull my fair share of the weight, and Aeberhard would be better off if I were to be replaced in my medical capacity."

"Do you want to be replaced?" she asked, stunned by this announcement. This clinic was his lifeblood. He'd die without it.

"Sometimes it's not a matter of what we want so much as what's best. I believe I should be replaced as a doctor, and I don't have the heart to take myself off my cases, so I'll leave that up to you."

"Maybe we could reduce your patient load," she suggested half-heartedly. She didn't want to get rid of Max. Not at all. She'd take more of him if there was any more to give, which, unfortunately, there was not. Sometimes the best doctoring wasn't about the medical care but about the heart that went with it, and Max was the heart here—the heart and soul.

"I'm not serving in the same manner as I've always required of everyone else. It's your responsibility, Catherine, to see that I do, or make other arrangements. And to that end, I do agree that the staff needs to be enlarged. As the owner, and I will still retain my rights of ownership, I'd like to see you increase our physician roster by another three to five members, for starters. And I'd also like to add your name to the title as part-owner of Aeberhard, so when the time comes, you'll have full authority to make the decisions I normally do."

That truly shocked her. So much so, in fact, that she staggered over to her desk and sat down in the mahogany-colored leather chair behind it. Speechless for a moment.

"I've thought about it for a while, and there's no one else I'd trust Aeberhard Clinic to. Not as much as I trust it to you."

Part-owner? She was still stunned. "Max, I…I couldn't. This is yours, all of it. You've worked hard…"

"And I'm getting on in years, a fact that's rather obvious these days."

A spark of panic grabbed her. "You're healthy, aren't you? There's nothing wrong?"

He chuckled. "I have a little arthritis in my knees, and my eyesight's not what it used to be. The rest of me is fine. Just getting…tired. And there are some things I want to do, Catherine. Places I want to see, books I want to read, friends I want to visit. It's time."

"So will you finally tell me why you chose me? A year ago, you sought me out and hired me, and now, when you're turning over part-ownership of your clinic to me, I still don't know, and I deserve an answer, Max. After all this time, you owe me that much."

"Yes, I do owe you, don't I?" He stepped away from the window, his slight limp a little more pronounced than usual, then studied her for a moment. "And, most likely, I'll tell you some time. When you're ready."

She thought about that for a moment, not so much frustrated by his response as puzzled. So much good fortune had come to her by way of this very dear man, yet she didn't know why and she'd never been up to demanding an answer. He was too kind, too generous. She didn't want to offend him, so once again she let it go. Briefly, though, as she thought about taking on more of the clinic responsibilities, an image of a sunny lemon grove flashed through her mind—a lemon grove and a villa sitting on top of a hill, overlooking it. But the reality of it came flooding back as she cast her gaze to the window, and the mountains just at the edge of the Aeberhard property line. This was home. She loved it here. "I'm honored, Max. I'll be glad to take on part-ownership. And as part-owner now, my first order of business is to convince you to stay on, in any capacity you wish." She turned to look at him. "However you want to practice, whenever you want to practice, I don't want you to resign. Take your holiday, go visit your friends, read your books, but come back to Aeberhard. We need you...I need you."

"We'll see," he said, on his way to the door. "And in the meantime, I've got to go have a look around Mrs Gunter's room to make sure she hasn't hidden any more candy with peanuts."

"Maybe over a weekend," Dante said, smiling as he felt the cozy warmth of this conversation spread through him. Talking with Gianni always did that. "I'll talk to your grandfather and see if he'll bring you here for a visit *this* weekend, if he doesn't have other plans." It tore him up every time he talked to Gianni, though. He needed to see his son. For someone who'd never expected to be a parent—at least, not for a very long time—being a father was as essential as the very air he breathed, and he thanked Dario every day for the privilege. It was like having a little bit of his brother still there with him. "In the meantime, tell Uncle Cristofor to set up an Internet connection so we can see each other when we talk."

"Can we do that?" Gianni squealed into the phone.

Laughing, Dante pulled the receiver away from his ear. "Tell him to get it set up then, when your grandfather brings you here for a visit, you can bring the equipment I'll need and we can set it up together at this end."

"Let me go and ask!" Gianni said, then dropped the phone and ran away, while Dante held on, waiting for him to return.

"Can I talk to you?" Catherine asked, poking her head in the door at that moment.

He nodded, motioning for her to enter. She took several steps into the room, then stopped when she saw that Dante was on the phone. "I'll come back," she offered, and started to turn away, but Dante stopped her.

"Don't go. I've been put on hold, and who knows how long this will take?"

She nodded. "It's about your therapy. Hans told me you refused a walker."

"Hans is correct. I refused." He hated the damned thing. Besides being ugly, it was a nuisance. Pick it up, move it forward then walk into it and start the whole process again. Hans and Catherine were lucky he hadn't thrown it out the window. "Too much trouble. Won't use it."

"Then what do you intend using?" she asked. "Because if you go from wheelchair to fully weight bearing, and your ankle snaps, your career is over. You'll require more pins to put your ankle back together, it will be permanently stiff this time, and you won't be able to drive if driving entails anything to do with your right foot. So tell me, Dante, what's your suggestion?"

He held out his hand to stop her talking, then listened into the phone. He could hear Gianni in the background, make out his voice but not what he was saying. Although he could guess. For eight, the boy was quite the little negotiator. He knew what it took to get his way, and most of the time he got it. That was Dario in him. Dario had been the smooth, charming one. A natural leader with a cheery disposition. People had loved him, adored him, given in to him because it had always been such a pleasure to do so. While he, on the other hand, was not…Dario. Gianni was, though, and Dante could hear him working his grandfather like the eight-year-old pro that he was.

When the voices trailed off, Dante turned his attention back to Catherine. "My suggestion is something other than a walker. You're the rehab doctor—I'll leave the decision up to you."

"And my decision is that I want you up bearing very little weight on a walker."

"Except the patient is refusing. I do have that right, you know." That, and he did enjoy arguing with Catherine. She positively glowed when she was antagonized.

"You know, Dante," she said, her voice filling with exasperation, "I'd have never slept with you if I'd known how stubborn you are. This is ridiculous. I know what's best for you yet you're refusing to listen to me, which puts me in the awkward position of recommending something that's second best. And I don't like it, not one little bit."

Yes, she positively glowed. "Something I remember from medical school, Catherine, is that patients do have rights in their medical decisions. I'm merely exercising mine not to agree with you. Don't take it personally."

"Personally? What would you do if one of the other doctors recommended a walker?"

"I'd give it all the consideration it was worth then refuse."

"So it's the walker? Not me?"

He shook his head. "I said don't take it so personally. I hate walkers, that's all. I sprained my knee a couple of years ago, refused the walker then and tottered around on crutches for a while. I do it pretty well."

"And you couldn't have mentioned that before?"

Rather than answering, Dante held out his hand again, waving it to silence her. "And what did he say?" he enquired into the phone.

"That he'll bring me to see you, and we can set up the computer. Cristofor also has a cell phone where you can take your picture and send it to me."

"You really want my picture?" he asked. It touched him that

Gianni missed him so much. "Don't you remember what I look like?"

"But you could change, Papa."

"I'm not changing. Promise."

"Can I bring the phone anyway?"

"Do you think you could ask Uncle Cristofor to get a phone for you, where you could take your picture for me?" Bad question. Gianni was already off in search of his uncle, leaving Dante to dangle on the other end of the line again. He chuckled, then looked at Catherine. "Gianni's eight. Very enthusiastic."

She nodded, but didn't respond. No expression on her face, not a hint of a smile, not even a frown. Which made him wonder.

"He said yes!" Gianni squealed into the phone, at which Dante, once again, pulled the receiver away from his ear. "Enthusiastic, and loud. Youthful exuberance," he whispered to Catherine, then turned his full attention to the phone call. Three minutes later, when Gianni had run out of stream, Dante saw that Catherine had slipped out of the room. He'd wanted to tell her about Gianni, but that would have to wait until later, he supposed. According to his schedule, it was time for lunch. Then off to have his hair cut, which actually didn't sound half-bad.

It was eight o'clock and Cathcrine was going home. Time to call it a day and get to bed at a decent hour for a change. She wasn't on call, didn't have a patient in dire need, and there was nothing to keep her in the clinic any longer. Tomorrow and all its headaches and triumphs would come soon enough. So Catherine bundled herself in to her wool coat, wrapped her cashmere scarf around her neck and headed directly to the nearest exit, her mind full of Max's decisions and Dante's refusal to follow orders. Most of all, her mind was on the child he'd called Gianni. Admittedly, she was bothered that Dante had a child, bothered that during the months they'd been together he'd never mentioned it to her. He could have been divorced, then. The time line was certainly right for that. Still, not to even mention a marriage or a relationship that had produced a child. And most of all not to mention a child...

But the way he'd talked to Gianni. She'd heard his voice, heard a tone from Dante she didn't recognize. Adoration was as close a way to describe it as she could think of. It had been more than Dante's voice, though. It had been the look in his eyes—an amazing look that told the whole story. Dante had a love in his life that was greater than anything she could even imagine and his eyes didn't hide the fact. Adoration again.

He was lucky to have that. For a time, during those weeks when they had been together, she'd wondered what it would be like to have his child. She hadn't been ready for a child, of course. They'd never even broached the subject. But it felt so odd that some woman had beat her to it—given him a son long before it had crossed her mind that she herself might want to have his child. In a way, she envied that woman. But she also feared for the child because Dante could turn out to be a wonderful father, or like her own father, who had always caused the family so much worry, who had always caused her family to live on the edge of a nervous breakdown. That was so difficult. So painful.

Catherine didn't wish that for anybody else.

Did Gianni's mother sit at home and worry about Dante the way her own mother had worried? Did she worry that the next race might bring about something worse than a broken ankle?

As Catherine slipped down the hall, past the entry to the solarium, a heavy blanket of gloom spread over her, thinking about all the times her own mother had sat at home, worrying. Those hadn't been happy days. Her mother had closed herself into a dark room and cried much of the time, then pretended everything was all right. But it never had been. They'd always lived with the fear, the distress. The unknown. Her mother had always said that a man like Emil Brannon should never have married and had children, and that a woman had to be crazy to fall in love with someone like him.

Her mother had always loved her father, though. Loved him like crazy, in spite of the worry and the hurt. But Catherine had suffered her own hurt, too, something that hadn't been part of her mother's. She'd been left out. Her mother had been so caught up with her own worry that she'd often turned her back on her daughter. And Catherine's father had been addicted to a lifestyle to which Catherine had never been admitted. So she'd grown up a lonely child. Then it had been too late. Her father had died and nothing could be changed.

Of course, going off and getting engaged to one man who had excluded her from matters important to her life then marrying another who was just like that seemed to be a pattern. One she would not repeat, especially now that she was better able to understand it and stop it from happening again.

As Catherine passed the solarium, she glanced in and saw that it was empty, apart from one figure sitting near the window, shrouded by the near-darkness. Catherine shivered when she saw him, knowing instinctively who it was. He'd always had that effect on her years ago, the one that caused shivers. Things hadn't changed much, and that was a problem. She truly didn't want to shiver over Dante any more. But her responses weren't altogether under her own control, which was another leftover from the past she'd have preferred not repeating.

For a moment she thought about stopping in to see him, then decided against it, and continued down the hall. But ten steps past the door she turned back and entered the solarium, forcing her steps to blend into the quite solitude of the place.

She didn't say a word as she approached him from behind, and he didn't flinch. But there was a keen awareness between them, something much more than the shiver running up her spine and gooseflesh rising on her arms. "Can I take you back to your room?" she finally whispered, for a lack of anything substantive to say.

"I like it here. Like to sit and look out. Back home, I have a large picture window where I like to sit and look out over my trees. The view is nothing like this, not nearly as spectacular, but it's nice there. A good place to return to after I've been on the road for a while." He turned his chair to face her. "Care to join me?"

"I'm not in the mood to argue, Dante. And that's all we do. How about I simply apologize for my behavior after you did Mrs Gunter's trach, tell you how sorry I am and how wrong I was, then leave before we start something else?"

"You're sorry?"

She nodded. "I was way out of line. But you don't exactly bring out the best in me."

"I've seen times when I've brought out the very best in you."

Catherine had the decency to blush over that comment. "Once in a while," she admitted. "But I got over you."

"And even got married."

"Yes, I even got married."

"And it was good for a while?"

"No, it wasn't ever good. He was set on one thing, I was set on another. He wanted children right away, almost before the honeymoon ended…wanted a typical family life. You know, a stay-at-home wife, someone domestic. A small detail we hadn't discussed before the wedding. And I couldn't fault him for what he wanted because it's a good life for someone else, but not for me as I didn't want any of what he did. So we ended the marriage before we did something foolish, like having a child. He married a few months later and has one child already, with another on the way."

"And you have your career. It seems you both must be happy, getting everything you wanted."

She pulled off the cashmere scarf and unbuttoned her coat.

But she wouldn't take it off because it was not her intention to stay. She wanted to, which was why she would not. "I took over part-ownership of the clinic today. We're going to expand, take on new doctors, offer new services. That's what makes me happy, Dante. So, yes, I did get everything I wanted."

"But are you happy enough, Catherine?" he asked. "I don't see any joy in your eyes, not the way I saw it when you were still a resident. All I see is…seriousness."

"Because I am serious, Dante. I think the Catherine you got to know back then was an anomaly, someone who really didn't exist." Or someone who had been happier for that brief time than she had ever been in her life before that. Even though that had been an illusion.

"Ah, but I believe she did exist—in flesh and blood and in spirit. She was an amazing woman, someone you should meet again. I think you'd like her."

"We make our choices, Dante. You made yours when you gave up medicine to be a race-car driver. I made mine when I took up the life I live now. And in a very real way I do believe that who we are dictates our choices as much as our choices dictate who we are."

"Then who were you when we slept together, Catherine?"

"A young woman who very much got caught up in the world of a dashing, exciting young surgeon."

"So all you wanted was a surgeon?"

"All I wanted was what I had."

He reached across and took her hand. "I wish it could have been more. Wish we'd had more time together."

"It was what it was, Dante." She didn't pull her hand from his. Rather, she remembered that touch, remembered that softness. It hadn't changed. But she had, and Dante was the reason. For that she thanked him, and cursed him. "A very nice time during a brief period of our lives. Like you said of your son earlier… youthful exuberance."

"Gianni," he said fondly, still holding onto her hand. "Everything I ever wanted."

"Why didn't you tell me you had a son, Dante? He would have been three when we were together. And you never mentioned him. Not a word. Nothing about his mother, either. Were you married then? Or now?"

"He's not my son, Catherine."

She frowned, clearly puzzled. "What?"

"He's Dario's son. My brother's. Dario's wife, Louisa, died a few weeks before Dario did—victim of a fast, virulent strain of pneumonia. I always thought he got back into the car to race too soon after that shock, which is part of what I think caused his accident. He was preoccupied, didn't have his power of concentration." He paused for a moment, a sad smile passing over his face. "Anyway, I lost my sister-in-law, then my brother, and took Gianni to live with me. He's my nephew, but I've adopted him as my son. And, no, I wasn't a married man, cheating on his wife. I've done a lot of things I'm not so proud of in my life, but I'd never do that."

"That's not fair. You told me practically nothing about your family. Nothing about yourself either, really. So how was I supposed to know anything?"

"Is there any point in going through this again?" His voice went thin with anger. "I did what I did, and there's no going back. You couldn't live with my choices, and I had to."

"Your choices for me, Dante," she flared. "That's what it was about. If I'd let you choose my life and come to you the way you wanted, would I have even known a child was involved before I got there? Or was me becoming a mother to your nephew another one of those things you'd have simply decided for me? Maybe let me find it out through another of your sister's premature announcements?"

"You couldn't live with someone who didn't want to be a doctor. That shattered your prefect image of what we were to become, and I do understand that, Catherine. That's why you're bitter."

"Bitter, Dante? Do you think I'm bitter?" He didn't understand, and that was the problem, then and now. It wasn't about the choice, it was about the lack of it, and she just didn't have the heart to go through the argument again.

The problem was, she could find herself right back in that same spot with him so easily. She'd known that the first instant she'd learned he was to be a patient there, and that feeling hadn't gone away as she'd hoped it might once she confronted him. If anything, she'd come to see this pull towards Dante as a flaw in herself—one that would make it so easy to go back to him over and over again, the same blind feelings on the line. Five years older, five years wiser in so many ways but this.

Apparently, five years were not enough for her, although one thing she did know with certainty—she couldn't afford the inevitable outcome of getting involved with Dante a second time. Yet the inevitable was so close if she'd allow it. One crook of the finger, one suggestive glance in his direction...

Catherine drew in a breath to brace herself. "Look, you're right. We don't need to go through all this again. What's done is done, and dwelling on it will just make us argue even more. I don't want to argue with you, Dante, so I've got to get going. I have...work to do at home."

"Are you sure you want to go?" he asked, his voice so low and utterly sexy she went weak in the knees. "Maybe we could have tea?"

Tea and whatever came with it. No, she wasn't sure she wanted to leave. Not sure at all. Which was why she pulled away from Dante altogether and walked to the door, taking care not to stagger from the sheer weight of what could have gone on between the two of them if she'd let it. For Dante it would have been just another night with another woman. She understood that about him more than she ever had before. But for her it would have been the start of another broken heart—a heart that had not yet mended fully from its first break, she'd just come to realize. "I'm sure, Dante. I'm very sure." Very sure, and very sad.

CHAPTER SIX

IT HAD been four days since Catherine had last talked to Dante in any way other than medical, and his progress was remarkable, all things considered. He was working hard at his therapy, motivated to push himself towards recovery. To get away from her? she wondered.

At this phase of his recovery her presence wasn't absolutely necessary unless something went wrong, and nothing was going wrong. So she stayed away from Dante as much as she could. That's the way it had to be in order to keep their personal differences out of his recovery. Which did concern her. Aggravation could hinder progress, and what they had going between them was definitely aggravating. She didn't want to impede his remarkable progress in any way.

"He's actually going to progress to a cane in another few days," Hans reported. "Very co-operative patient now. I wish everyone worked as hard as Dante does."

Very co-operative for everyone but her. Dante was playing on that, damn him. Even when they weren't together, he ended up taking control of every speck of her thoughts. Controlled her thoughts, dictated so many of her movements. Dante Baldassare was creeping his way in, and she lacked the will to defend herself. Did that mean she wanted it? No, of course not! She didn't, couldn't...absolutely not! "Very co-operative," Catherine repeated breathlessly, trying to put the other thought out of her mind. "So, what's your estimate on his length of stay here, taking into consideration his current level of progress?" Was tomorrow too soon to rush him out the door? she wanted to ask, even though she knew better.

"Another couple of weeks, at the most," Hans replied. "Probably a few days less than that. He's coming along well, but he's not ready to get back into any type of typical physical routine yet, which is what will happen once he's out of here. Especially with his race schedule for next season. So I think he needs more healing time because of his lifestyle factors."

She nodded, feigning interest in the same page of Dante's chart she'd been staring at for the past five minutes. Another two weeks with Dante? She wasn't sure how she was going to endure it. "If he's ready to advance, let's increase his therapy by one more session a day. Include some strength training in that, and progress him from the crutches he's using to a quadcane before he goes to a regular cane. And don't let him talk you into anything else." She hastily scribbled those orders in the chart, snapped it shut and handed it back to the medical clerk on that ward. "I'll try and have a look at him before lunch." Not that she wanted to, but it was her medical duty.

"He's free right now," Hans suggested. "We've already done his morning session, and I've left him in his room. If you're not busy now…"

Nothing like being cornered. "Fine. Let's go."

Hans shook his head. "Can't. Dante's free, I'm not." With that, he trotted off to his next patient, leaving Catherine standing in the hall, looking for someone to buffer her next meeting with Dante. But no one was available.

"You're being silly," she muttered as she drug herself to Dante's room, resisting each and every step along the way. "Just plain silly."

"I am not!" came the tentative little voice from around the corner.

Catherine stopped first, then took two steps forward and peeked around that corner, at the little boy standing there. Young, probably seven or eight, he had black hair a little on the curly side, deep blue eyes that would be lady-killers in another few years and a grin she recognized almost immediately. He could only be Dante's nephew, but if this was Gianni, he was the image of his uncle. "You're not being silly?" she asked him, trying to keep a straight face. The child was already melting her heart, the way he was looking up at her. Dante's eyes, Dante's charm.

"No. It's silly, being silly. I'm not supposed to be."

"Why is it silly?" she asked him.

He shrugged. "I don't know."

She finally gave in to a laugh. "Then I suppose it's a good thing I was the one who was being silly and not you, since you're not supposed to be."

"What were you doing that was silly?" he asked.

"Being afraid of someone I shouldn't be afraid of."

"Why?" he asked

She exaggerated a big frown for him, then huffed out a dramatic breath. "I don't know." Gianni's serious expression softened, and so did her heart even more. "I guess that is being pretty silly, isn't it?"

"That's OK. My papa says sometimes you have to be a little silly. That it makes you feel better." Finally, he grinned at her. "As long as you're not silly all the time. Are you?"

"Am I silly all the time?"

Gianni nodded.

"Only when I have to be." She held out her hand to him. "And your papa is right. Sometimes it does make you feel better. My name's Catherine Wilder. And you are?"

"Gianni Baldassare," he said in all seriousness as he shook Catherine's hand.

"Well, it's a pleasure to meet you, Gianni. Welcome to Aeberhard."

"I'm spending the night here," he boasted. "With my papa. He said I could."

"Does he know where you are right now?"

Gianni blushed. "He was busy with Uncle Cristofor and Papa Marco. I went for a walk and I, um…"

"Are you lost?"

He nodded, a slight blush creeping into his cheeks. "Just a little. I thought this was where his suite is, but it isn't."

She held out her hand to the boy. "I know you probably aren't supposed to go with strangers, but your father and I are friends. How about I take you back to his room and sneak you in so he'll never know that you got lost?"

There wasn't a scrap of reluctance in the way Gianni latched onto her hand, and he held tight to her as they walked down the hall to Dante's suite. He did hang back a little at the door, however. Anticipating punishment, perhaps? Or reluctant to admit a mistake?

Catherine bent down and whispered, "Here's the plan, Gianni. I'll go in first and start talking to your father. That will distract him, then you can sneak in. Go and sit in the little room off to the side of the entrance and he'll never know you were gone." A brilliant plan if you were a child, but Dante would see, as he should. It would be interesting to watch the way he dealt with the boy.

Gianni nodded, pleased with the plan. "Thank you," he whispered back, then did a most unexpected thing. He gave her a quick kiss on her cheek. Like Dante would do. Actually, like Dante had done on more than one occasion. Had Gianni learned it from Dante—seen Dante do it to other women?

Catherine knocked lightly on the door, waited a moment then entered, taking care to leave the door behind her slightly ajar. As she entered the room, she glanced back once at the cute little face looking in. Dante was a lucky man. Very lucky. "I need to have a look at your ankle," she announced as she moved forward into the main part of the suite. "I've approved you for an extra therapy session every day to help you get your strength back and left an order with Hans to progress you to the quad cane, and I want to make sure you're ready for the advancement." She nodded to Cristofor, whom she recognized instantly, glanced briefly at Dante, and immediately fixed her stare on the one she thought was Papa Marco. An older, silver-haired version of Dante. One thing was for sure. The Baldassare men, from the youngest to the oldest, had their fair share of good looks. Lady-killers, one and all. "You're all welcome to stay. This won't take a minute."

"Quad cane?" Dante asked, shaking his head. "Not me. I'll use a regular cane, or walk without one."

"And risk reinjury. That's your choice, Dante. If you don't want to drive next season…"

"You do like the doctor tells you!" Dante's father piped up. "If she says you need this quad cane, you need this quad cane."

Catherine immediately liked the older Baldassare. The man was loud, the man was genuine.

"He gives everybody a hard time this way," Marco said, extending his hand to Catherine. "I'm Marco, and you must be Dr Wilder. Cristofor has told me all about you."

Cristofor, not Dante. That caused an unexpected lump in her throat. Nobody in Dante's family had ever known about their relationship, their engagement. Suddenly she felt excluded again. "Nice to meet you, Mr Baldassare." She took his hand. Nice grip. Soft. But not soft life Dante's. A flash of Dante's hands the first time she'd felt them on her caught her off guard, and she physically shook her head to rid herself of that image.

"Call me Marco. Everybody does." He twisted to give Dante an exuberant smile and a big wink of approval, then returned his attention to Catherine. "So, if he does his therapy the way you want him to, when can he drive?"

"As in competitively?" she asked, knowing that's what he meant. "Or for his own personal transportation? Because right now, if he doesn't follow my orders, his driving will be limited to a wheelchair, and for that, he's ready right now."

Marco threw back his head and laughed, then pulled Catherine into his arms and gave her a big hug. "I like this doctor, Dante. She can keep up with you." He released her, then stepped back for an appraisal. "And she looks good, too. Almost as good as your mama when I first met her. Now, that was a good-looking woman!"

"Papa, I don't think…" Dante started, but something behind Catherine caught his attention, and he stopped. Then he looked up at her. "Is there something going on I should know about?"

"Such as?" she asked, still a little overwhelmed by Marco's enthusiastic greeting.

Dante lowered his voice. "Such as why my son is sneaking in behind you?"

Catherine shook her head. "No, there's nothing to know. Nothing at all."

"And I can trust that?"

She nodded. "You can trust that, Dante."

He thought about that for a moment, then nodded. "Fine. So, do your exam." Dante's chosen chair was a recliner near the window. He forced the recliner back until his ankle was sufficiently elevated for Catherine's examination, then shut his eyes. "Thank you," he whispered.

"For what?"

"Protecting Gianni's dignity. It's not easy being his age, living the life we do. It's good he found a champion to protect him."

"What would you have done to him otherwise?"

He chuckled. "Nothing nearly so frightening as he was anticipating. Fearing the punishment is often worse than the punishment itself."

"He's great, Dante. You're doing a good job with him."

"He's doing a good job with me. I love being his father." He studied her for a moment, then smiled. "See? This isn't so bad between us, is it?"

Rather than answering Dante, Catherine removed his shoe, then his sock, and had a look at his ankle. On the exterior it seemed fine. No unusual swelling, no redness. The scars were healing nicely—he had two major scars from the surgeries and several tiny ones from the injury itself. "What caused these?" she asked, running her fingertips over the small ones to make sure they were not hot to the touch.

"The car was on fire," Marco offered. "Dante got out before it exploded, but his ankle was broken and he had to drag himself across the road."

"But you weren't burned?" she asked, an image of the accident now forming. Car crashed, Dante injured, trying to escape the fire. It could have so easily gone the other way. Car crashed, Dante injured, not able to escape the fire. That thought caused her hands to tremble, and she immediately withdrew them from his foot.

"Fire retardant suit," Dante said. "That, and the fact that even with a broken ankle I can be pretty damned fast when I have to be."

All three Baldassare men laughed at that remark, but Catherine didn't find it funny in the least. If anything, she was sickened even more by what she'd heard—sickened that they were taking it all so lightly. "And the fact is, running on your ankle like you had to do may well be the reason the injury was so bad initially. Of course, not following doctor's orders, like you've been doing, hasn't helped. And if you want my opinion, you'll be lucky to get a full range of motion back if you mess up again." Or go through another car crash.

"Don't need a full range. Just enough so I can drive again," he riposted, although he sounded more serious about it than she'd expected. Men like Dante shrugged these things off.

Sustain an injury, move on. Sustain another injury, risk your life, move on.

"And that's all there is?" she snapped, not intending to. It just slipped out and she couldn't help it. "Driving? You escape with your life once, and you can't wait to get back into your car and tempt fate yet another time?" She shook her head in disgust. "I thought you valued life more than that, Dante! For someone who went to school to preserve life, you've become reckless…irresponsible with your own."

"And you care?" He pushed up in the chair and gave his father and brother the signal to leave the room. But Catherine turned, trying to leave before them. He grabbed her by the hand and held onto her, though. Held on tight until they were alone. "What the hell is this about, Catherine?" he snapped.

"I don't know what you're talking about."

"Your lecture. Your attitude. Both are uncalled for, not to mention the fact that what I do with my life is none of your business."

"Your brother getting killed wasn't a wake-up call, Dante? Because it should have been."

"My brother getting killed was one of the unfortunate consequences of racing. It happens. We know that. It's always a tragedy. But it wasn't a wake-up call. When you step into the car you take on the risk…"

"Of getting killed. I understand that, Dante." As a doctor. Especially as a daughter. She'd been the child who'd lived with the fear of those risks. Every day, every night. Just like Gianni did. Dear God, her heart went out to the child. "But what I don't understand is why. And I don't understand how you could give up such a noble position in medicine to…to take those risks." She wrenched her hand from his grasp. "And what about Gianni?"

"Gianni understands racing."

"For God's sake, Dante," she cried. "He's just a little boy. How can he understand anything?" At that age, she hadn't. She'd lived with the fear but had never understood why until she had been much older. Which was when she'd started loathing the reason.

"Catherine, what's this about? What's this really about?"

She drew in a deep breath, trying to regain control. He was right. *This was none of her business.* Her responsibility here was to heal him. That's all. She had no claims, no right to any emotions other than what a patient's physician might feel. And the way she was acting…silly, and not one of those moments when Dante had told Gianni it was OK to be silly. "What this is about is a doctor who's concerned that the next time her patient is involved in a car crash, he'll injure his ankle again, possibly to the point that it can't be fixed."

"You're lying," he accused, but in a gentle tone.

A tone that had always melted her. She refused to look into his eyes because what she would see would melt her even more. "No, Dante. I'm not. As a doctor, you know that what I'm saying could be the truth. You don't think like a doctor any more, however."

"Maybe that's the case, but that's not what this has been about, Catherine, even if you're not willing to admit it." He glanced around Catherine as Gianni finally crept into the room. Gianni, whose eyes never left Catherine. "And what have you been doing with yourself this past hour?" he asked, even though the answer was clear on the boy's face.

"Just sitting," he said, then pointed to the anteroom. "In there."

"That's all?"

"I…I met Catherine," he said, taking care not to divulge the particulars.

Dante glanced up at Catherine, a seductive smile crossing his lips. "My son has excellent taste in women. Women who have a fierce need to protect the men they care for, it seems. Do you think that woman would care to join two of the Baldassare men for dinner tonight—here, in the suite? I understand there is an excellent caterer in the village. Brilliant pastries. Are you still a vegetarian?"

This was the way he always did it. He'd get her worked up, then do something nice, something totally unexpected to catch her off guard. But tonight would be safe, having Gianni there. Admittedly, the thought of a pleasant evening with Dante did seem appealing. Of course, it would be a good way to get their doctor-patient relationship back on track. Talk out the rough patches, work out the details. At least, that's what she was telling herself when she accepted.

"Around seven?" Dante said. "I know it's a little early, but one of the Baldassare men has an eight o'clock bedtime."

"Around seven," Catherine repeated, then turned and made a rather hasty departure, hoping her shaky knees didn't give way before she was out in the hall.

"OK, so I knew her in Boston," Dante admitted to his father. They'd been arguing the subject of Catherine Wilder for the past ten minutes and his father wasn't going to give up until Dante made a confession.

"And how did you know her?" Marco asked, a very knowing smile sliding to his lips.

"We were medical colleagues. Worked in the same hospital."

"Baldassare men aren't *just* colleagues with beautiful women like that. And that one…she has passion, Dante. Feisty eyes. That's where the passion shows. It's for you, perhaps?"

"It's for her work. She's driven. Doesn't want a home, doesn't want a family. All she wants is her job." He didn't remember that hardness in her before but, admittedly, there were a great many things he'd failed to notice about Catherine back then. His loss.

"But a Baldassare man can always make a woman change her mind, eh?"

Except for Catherine. There wasn't a Baldassare man alive who could penetrate that steely fortress, if she didn't want it penetrated. But he wasn't going to tell that to his father. It would simply give the old man more of a reason to pursue Catherine as a future daughter-in-law. Which was something that wasn't going to happen. "A Baldassare man can always make a woman change her mind *if* the Baldassare man wants to change her mind," he said, hoping that would be the end of the discussion. But he was wrong.

"Tell me why he wouldn't…why *you* wouldn't."

"We don't get along, Papa. That's all there is to it. Catherine and I do not get along. And we don't want the same things."

"But I see that look in her eyes…in your eyes."

"It's called frustration, anger."

Marco laughed. "If I didn't know better, I might think you were not my son. Baldassare men are wiser than that where a good woman is concerned. So I think you're trying to fool yourself. Or fool that lady doctor."

"I think I'm trying to have a conversation about car modifications that can give us better traction when the course is slippery." He glanced over at Cristofor, who'd positioned himself in the corner in a chair, reading a racing magazine and purposely avoiding the discussion about Catherine. "Which is your department," he said to his brother.

"Getting better traction on a slippery course?" Cristofor smiled. "Or in a slippery relationship?

"Gianni's still swimming," Dante said as Catherine entered the suite. "One of the physical therapy aids took him to the pool a little while ago and I'm afraid that our company, compared to playtime in the swimming pool, didn't merit a second thought. But he did say to tell the nice lady hello."

It was the same suite she'd been in hundreds of times, with dozens of different patients. Yet tonight, with Dante, it looked different, more intimate, more…more the place of something other than a casual meal with an old friend, a former lover, a colleague, a patient, or whatever Dante was to be considered. The lights were dimmed. The music playing in the background was faint...Tchaikovsky, she thought. Champagne was chilling, crudités of Belgian endive, teardrop tomatoes, blanched asparagus, fennel bulbs and red peppers were chilled and waiting with a balsamic dip. And if she wasn't mistaken...She inhaled deeply. "Is that eggplant involtini? And foccacia with savory and picholine olives?" He remembered her favorite meal. They'd dined on it at a little Italian restaurant not far from her flat a few days before he'd left her. "You didn't have that catered here," she said, fighting with herself to remain unaffected. The truth was, a good eggplant involtini had gotten Dante everything he'd wanted on more than one occasion. Was that what he had in mind now? Gianni was gone for the evening so bring in the food he knew could seduce her?

"Baldassares have friends everywhere. I know a good chef not far from here..."

"One who's sure to cook the meal that will seduce me into bed," Catherine snapped. "Is that what this is about, Dante? Do you want to conquer me again? Once wasn't enough for you?"

He tried to look hurt, tried to look concerned, but it simply did not work. The Dante Baldassare who had seduced her, even more than the eggplant involtini, had broken through, and he held out his hand in gesture for her to sit. "The only thing I want to conquer tonight is a good meal, and a good champagne to celebrate being together again. I'd like to think that we could be friends, Catherine."

"Except that we're not together," she insisted, refusing to accept his invitation to be seated. "Not in the sense you want to be."

"How do you know what I want?" he asked.

"Fame, fortune, women...doesn't that about say it all?" She'd read the celebrity magazines from time to time, seen his picture with various different women. Beautiful women. Women who knew their way around the life he lived now. Not women like her, who only knew their way around a medical chart.

He chuckled. "That does say some of it, I'll admit. I do like the lifestyle, Catherine. I won't lie to you about it, or pretend it's not a part of me, because it is. Always has been. When I was young, I was a part of it because of my family. It was theirs and I reaped the benefits. But now I have that lifestyle on my own because of what I've done, and I'm not going to apologize or make excuses."

"You used to have so many expectations about medicine, Dante, and the kind of life you would have as a doctor. What happened to those?"

"Those were expectations of a life that didn't come to be."

"I always thought that life would have made you happy."

"It would have," he said, his voice giving over to a little melancholy. "I think I might have been a good surgeon, and I did want that."

"Doesn't it make you sad that you gave it all up? Don't you ever miss it? I mean, I don't know what I'd do if I had to quit medicine." She'd wither away. What she did defined who she was. Some might think that was too consuming, but it was the way she chose to live her life, and if she was too consumed, so be it.

Dante thought for a moment, the grin that had been on his face suddenly vanishing. "Sometimes it does make me a little sad. I liked being a doctor, and every now and then I think about going back to it someday, when I'm finally too old to climb into a race car. But I don't know if that will happen. My father is getting older and with his heart condition he'll need someone to run his part of Baldassare Racing one day. And so many people depend on the racing team as a livelihood. It's a prosperous enterprise, with dozens of people working for us. A lot of responsibility to lot of people." He shrugged. "I'd be happy being a surgeon, or even a country doctor, but sometimes we don't get everything we want, do we?"

"So we make the best of what we have," she finished for him. As a child, that had been her life. Been her mother's life, too. Always making the best of things. "But you'd be a doctor again, if you could?" That did surprise her, but yet, remembering the Dante Baldassare she'd once known, it did not. He'd wanted to be a doctor more than anything else, and maybe there was some of that desire still lingering in him.

"I've never *not* been a doctor, Catherine. From the day I received my certificate, I've always been a doctor. Just not one actively practicing." He gestured again for her to sit. "And having Gianni with me, the one thing I've learned more than anything is that the happiness we have in life is not about the things surrounding it but the people in it. The rest of it doesn't matter so much. Now, are you going to join me?"

"And Gianni?" she asked.

"He talked about you this afternoon, about the new friend he met in the hall. He liked you, said you are a very nice lady. I thought about teaching him the meaning of accomplice, since you sneaked him back in the room when I'd told him not to go out." Dante wheeled over to pull the chair out for Catherine. "But I got into trouble myself when I was that age, and that's part of the growing-up process—learning to get yourself out of your messes. Being resourceful, which he was."

Catherine laughed. "Yes, he was. He's just like you, Dante." Dante as a father—it was a new concept for her, but one that fitted him well. He was a good father who saw reason on both sides. He would inspire confidence in Gianni. Unfortunately, like her father had done, she feared he would also inspire the cold, down-to-the-marrow kind of fear that wouldn't go away.

"He convinced me that taking a swim is a healthy thing to do, so what could I say? The boy's persuasive. Didn't he persuade you to protect him in his little adventure?"

"He's like you," she said again as she sat down, taking care not to brush up against Dante. This had to be a meal with distance. That was the only way she could get through it. "Always breaking the rules. And always so charming when trying to fix his messes. I think it must be a natural gift for the Baldassare men."

Dante uncorked the champagne, poured two flutes full, and handed one over to her. As much as she tried not to brush her hand against his as she took it, his fingers did slide ever so gently across the back of her hand, causing her to suck in a razor-sharp breath. For a moment she felt fire, felt the tingle of a wild spark ignite the flesh on the back of her hand and spread up her arm.

She wanted to be calm about this, wanted to force her face to remain expressionless, but if Dante still owned the powers of observation he had all those years ago, then he'd already noticed her subtle reaction to him. He'd seen the slight shiver, understood the barely perceptible recoil. Maybe even felt her pulse quicken. He was polite not to mention it, however, even though, when she finally risked a glance at him, he was staring at her, his eyes penetrating something far deeper than her skin. "I…um…I like him," she finally managed to force out. "Like I…um…mentioned earlier, you're doing a good job…um…raising him."

"I didn't make you *this* nervous the very first time we went out," he said. His voice was so quiet it nearly blended into the shadowed ambience. "In fact, I thought you were pretty bold for an American woman, going to bed with me on that first night."

"Bold?" she asked, recalling that evening. They'd known each other six hours and for five and a half of those hours she'd babbled on about things he cared nothing about, giggled over things that weren't funny, and spilled white wine in his lap. She didn't remember any part of that as being bold. "I call it being a twit. I don't normally do things like that." First time, only time. After Dante, she'd been overly cautious. In fact, she'd dated Robert Wilder for nearly three months before she'd even allowed him the first kiss. The rest had come on their wedding night, which definitely hadn't been the mark of a very bold woman, since the pace of their relationship had been all her choice.

"But a cute twit." Dante placed the champagne bottle back on ice then held up his flute for a toast. "Here's to being a twit," he said, leaning over to chink his glass against hers. "The sexiest twit I've ever known."

"You only say that because you want me now and you know you can't have me," she said as she moved the flute to her lips. She smiled as the champagne bubbled up to tickle her nose. "And you're remembering what you'll never have again."

"You think I want you?" He arched a playful eyebrow.

Rather than answering right away, she sipped the champagne, enjoyed the taste of pure luxury on her tongue for a moment. Honestly, she was the one who wanted him, a fact that sipping champagne with him only heightened. "Of course you want me," she finally replied, trying to ignore the real truth of it all, hoping she wasn't being too obvious about it or giving herself away. "Or else, why all this?" She gestured to the beautifully set table and the elegant food that had been catered.

"To spend an evening with an old friend, perhaps?"

"We were many things to each other, Dante, but I'm not sure you could count being friends among them. You never even told your family about me, or about our engagement."

"Because I wanted you to be there. I knew they would love you and I wanted you to be part of the celebration. That's all it was. Not some contrived plot or exclusion. I like the new, sharper edge to you, Catherine. It becomes you. But the distrust doesn't."

"If I seem distrustful, that's because it's necessary. I've come a long way in a short amount of time, and it would be easy to become vulnerable. Where I am, what I'm doing…there's no place for vulnerability, the way I used to be vulnerable. And I was, Dante. We both know that."

But your vulnerability was always one of the nicest parts of you."

She thought about that for a moment, then shook her head. "No, it was then, but it's not now. Unless you're someone who wants to take advantage of me."

"There's no reason to suspect me of anything because I never wanted to take advantage of you, Catherine. I've always thought that what we had together was good for us both. Was I wrong about that?"

"You weren't wrong, Dante. It was good. Maybe better than anything I expected. Or wanted."

"So you married a man who wasn't what you expected or wanted, and he broke your heart?"

No, her husband hadn't been the one to break her heart. But she would never say that to Dante. "Should we wait for Gianni to come back before we eat, because the aroma of the eggplant involtini is making me ravenous?"

The sooner she ate, the quicker she could leave. Something she thought necessary, as her feelings right now weren't that different from what they had been that first night they'd dined together. And look what had happened then!

CHAPTER SEVEN

DINNER WAS a lackluster affair, and their conversation throughout was largely kept off anything personal. They talked about the clinic and the work that was being done there, the surrounding countryside, various old colleagues from Boston. All of it was very polite, all very neutral, almost to the point of being clinical. It certainly wasn't what he'd expected from his evening. No, he hadn't planned on their brief time together turning into anything like they'd had before. But he'd expected much more than this.

He thought back to their first evening…he hadn't planned on it being romantic for a first date, but what he'd got had been a shocker. No candles and soft music. No champagne and caviar. He recalled pizza, no meat to suit Catherine's vegetarian diet. And white wine…from her paper cup into his lap. They'd eaten out of the cardboard box, cross-legged on the floor, looking across the coffee-table at each other. Her medical texts books had been spread out everywhere, as had medical journals and magazines. Her flat had been testament to the fact that she was serious about what she did, and Catherine had literally taken her hand and brushed a stack of books off the coffee-table so they could eat. Brushed them right off onto the floor onto a pile of other books. And he'd loved it! Loved that spontaneity.

But Catherine's wall had been up from the moment she'd walked into his suite this evening until the moment she'd walked away, never relaxing even a little. Such a disappointment, although he'd told himself he had no expectations. That he was as wrong for her as her husband had been.

Now it was an hour after that ordeal was over, and Dante was left to wonder why he'd even bothered.

"It couldn't have been that bad," Marco said, sitting back in the overstuffed wingback near the window in Dante's suite. He was eating leftovers from the crudités Catherine had barely touched—a culinary offering not easy to find at this time of the year in an area such as this. Especially the Belgian endive and the fennel bulbs. Her favorites. Odd tastes, but Dante had remembered that, and he'd hoped Catherine might at least have mentioned it. She'd regarded that effort with all the interest of someone choosing an ordinary cracker out of a tin, though, and hurried on to the main course.

Talk about a hint. Nobody had to hit Dante over the head with a plate of eggplant involtini to make that message perfectly clear. She hadn't wanted to be there, and to prove that, she'd come and gone in less than an hour. And now his father was reaping the benefits of a meal Dante had thought would break a little of the ice between him and Catherine.

"It was worse. She ate three bites, then left. And I think if she could have eaten less and got out of here quicker, she would have."

"And where was that Baldassare charm? I've seen you charm the ladies, Dante. You don't have to work so hard to get what you want. It was only, what, three months ago, that you had that hot little duchess hanging on your arm? She would have appreciated this evening you laid out for Dr Wilder, and been eager to show her appreciation." He took a bite of the endive and turned up his nose. "Appreciated everything, except this."

"She wasn't a duchess. She was a distant relative of one. The third cousin of a third cousin."

"OK, OK, so not a duchess. But she had a royal lineage and

she was definitely interested in your lineage, among other things." He gave his eyebrows a wicked arch. "A Baldassare man knows these things without being told." Tossing the endive back on the tray, he shook his head. "Or he should, but I'm beginning to wonder about you."

"She was twenty-one, Papa. I was old enough to be her—"

"Lover," Marco supplied, his eyes twinkling as he dragged one of the teardrop tomatoes through the balsamic dip, popped it in his mouth, then nodded his head in approval. After he'd swallowed, he continued, "And the one before that…she was that famous author. Best-seller lists, Dante. Your mama has read her books, and let me tell you, the way that woman writes those sexy love scenes…they make your mama blush. You should be so lucky to have a woman like that author."

"I was research for her," Dante quipped. "Racing research," he clarified quickly. "For another book she's writing."

"It doesn't matter why. All that matters is that you had your chance with her, like you had your chance with the duchess, and with all those others, any one of them begging to be a Baldassare woman. And here you are, going crazy over the one who must be crazy herself for not wanting you. It doesn't make sense, Dante." Marco faked a shudder. "She must not understand what it is to be wanted by a Baldassare."

"Actually, I think she does understand. Which is why she wants no part of it. Or us."

Marco turned a quizzical stare on his son. "Which is why you want her, no? It's always such a challenge, isn't it, to want the one you can't have?"

Dante shook his head without answering.

"When you had an affair with this woman…" Marco started, but Dante held out his hand to stop him.

"I've never said anything about having an affair with Catherine," he snapped.

"Let me finish before you snap at me again. What I was trying to say was that, when you had an affair with this woman—and you did have an affair with her, Dante, I can see it in the way you two look at each other— I believe it was an affair of the heart. I believe you fell in love with her. Am I wrong?"

"How long did it take for you to fall in love with Mama?" Dante asked, partly because he wanted to know and partly because he wanted to avoid answering the question. It was too complicated, too loaded with emotions he didn't want to feel again.

"I fell in love with your mama in the time it takes to blink. I saw her, I blinked my eyes to make sure I wasn't dreaming, and when I looked again she had my heart. Is that how it is with you, Dante? Because Baldassare men are very passionate that way when they find the one they love. It grabs on, and doesn't let go." He grinned. "Baldassare men are born with hot blood!"

Dante had blinked that first time he'd laid eyes on Catherine. Oh, how he'd blinked. Although he wasn't sure how hard. The problem was, Catherine hadn't blinked. Not then. Not now. And it didn't make a bit of difference how passionate this particular Baldassare man was when he fell in love—the woman didn't love him back. Maybe she might have all those years ago, if only in a very small way. But he'd ruined that completely, and now she was making it perfectly clear that nothing from that time had smoldered, waiting to rekindle again. Nothing at all.

So much for the Baldassare charm.

"Have you looked in on Gianni tonight?" Cristofor asked, stepping out of the smaller guest room in the suite, where he'd been checking on the boy. "He seems a little warm."

"He had a good workout in the pool," Dante commented. "He was a little cranky when I helped him get ready for bed an hour ago, but nothing out of the ordinary. I think he was tired. Lots of exercise combined with being away from his normal routine."

"Except the boy doesn't have a normal routine," Marco snorted over a helping of the eggplant involtini.

Dante regarded his father for a moment, opened his mouth to say something but instead answered Cristofor. "This is the way he acts when he's tired. Nothing to be concerned over."

"Except that he's restless. Tossing and turning. Throwing off his covers."

"He's probably catching a cold," Marco offered as he poured himself a glass of champagne. "It's a wonder he doesn't get sick more often, with all the things he's exposed to when he's not at home." He took a sip, savored it for a moment, decided it was good then went back for a second, larger sip before he spoke again. "When I raced, you boys were raised in a proper home with a good mother taking care of you. I didn't allow all this running around the way you do, Dante. All over the world, never sleeping in the same bed…" He clucked his tongue. "God only knows what kind of food that boy is eating. Probably something to make him sick like he is now."

Again, Dante fought back the urge to reply. They'd had this argument before. Get married and give Gianni a real home, traditional life. Tired, old arguments and most of the time Dante merely turned a deaf ear. Sometimes, though, that wasn't so easy.

"Children get sick, Papa," Cristofor interjected. "I don't think it matters where they are. It happens."

"But maybe not so much if they…"

Instead of staying there listening to the same things he'd heard dozens of times before, Dante spun around and wheeled into the guest room, straight over to the bed, where Gianni was, indeed, tossing and turning. "You feeling OK?" he asked, as he laid the back of his hand across Gianni's forehead. Definitely hot. Not burning up, but hot enough that his skin was a little damp.

Gianni nodded, but didn't answer.

"Mind if I take a look at you?" Dante asked, taking hold of Gianni's wrist to feel for a pulse. Quite normal. So were his lymph glands, Dante discovered as he prodded below Gianni's jaw. No discomfort in his belly, either. Skin was fine. Eyes were fine. It was a little frustrating that he couldn't do a better examination, but come morning, if Gianni wasn't feeling better, he'd get Catherine to take a closer look. Or loan him the instruments so he could do it himself.

Ten minutes later, after a favorite bedtime story, Gianni finally drifted off to sleep. Dante returned to the main room of the suite, shutting the bedroom door behind him. "He'll be fine," he said.

"I think we should call one of the doctors here," Marco countered. "Let them have a look."

Dante gave him an odd look, and drew in a sharp breath. "I'm a doctor," he said, gritting his teeth. It may have been a while since he'd practiced, but he was certainly still capable of diagnosing a simple case of too much excitement. After good night's sleep Gianni would feel better in the morning. There wasn't a doubt in his mind about this, or he would have called another doctor.

"But not for a long time," his father argued. "I think we should—"

Enough of this. He was tired of it, and at the rate things were deteriorating between him and his father, he was afraid he'd say something he'd regret later on. So better to end the evening now, before that happened. "I think you should go to your hotel," Dante said, fighting for self-control. "And leave Gianni's care up to me."

"The boy needs a home, Dante. I've told you that before. Home, stability…a mother. Someone like that Dr Wilder. I know you love him, but dragging him around with you everywhere the way you do…"

"And what would you have me do? Give up racing?" And marry Catherine? She didn't want children. Hell, she didn't want home or stability, either. But there was no point arguing that with his father. "I gave up one career already, Papa. Isn't that enough for you?"

Cristofor stepped up behind Dante and laid a hand on his shoulder. "It's been a long day," he said. "I think a good night's sleep is what we all need."

Cristofor, always the diplomat in the rather opinionated, stubborn family. And the Baldassare family was all that, and more. Close, loving, and always very outspoken about what they wanted. Dante lifted a hand to pat his brother's, and nodded. "I think you're right. How about we make it a late morning tomorrow—that will give Gianni time to rest. Maybe meet in the solarium at noon?"

Marco gave a grudging nod of his head and stormed out the door. Cristofor lingered behind. "You know he doesn't mean anything by that, don't you?"

"Sometimes it's hard to know what he means," Dante said. "He'd have me married only because Gianni needs a mother. But I'm not ready to rush down the aisle only for the sake of…well, it would only be for the sake of pleasing Papa, wouldn't it, as I'm not keen on getting married just yet?"

"He'd have you married because he wants to see you happy, Dante. I think he worries as much about you as he does Gianni because you don't have much of a life for yourself. Which, you don't."

"I'm a good…father." Sometimes it still felt odd to say that, because he was not the boy's father, and he did want Gianni to remember that he'd had a father. Although Gianni had no recollection of Dario other than what Dante had told him.

"You are. And the way you raise him works fine for both of you. For now. But Gianni's still young. Children that age don't have so many needs. Still, you've got to realize that he's growing up, Dante. Think about how you were where you were a little older than Gianni is now. Think about the things you did, the things you counted on in your life—regular school, regular friends, the same bed every night. You always had that. No matter how busy Papa was, no matter how often he traveled, we always had the things Papa wants for Gianni. So don't get angry with him because, in his heart, he means well. But he's…" Cristofor laughed "—a Baldassare."

"You're the baby of the family," Dante said. "You shouldn't be the smartest." Admittedly, all those things Cristofor said did worry him, too. He'd thought about them more than once. But there wasn't a good solution right now. Not if he wanted to stay on the race circuit, which he did. After all, he'd started late trying to make it through the ranks, from the small circuits to the top, where he was now. Now that he was where he needed to be, there weren't so many racing years ahead of him. That was always the consolation. There was plenty of time ahead, after he quit driving. But then Dario would always come to mind, and he'd wonder if his brother had thought the same thing. *Always enough time*. The truth was, for the things in life you wanted and loved most, there was never enough time, and it didn't matter if you stepped into a race car every day or a surgical theater. "You go and calm Papa down," Dante said. "I'm sure he needs it. And I'll see you both tomorrow." He chuckled. "If he's speaking to me by then."

Cristofor laughed. "He gets angry fast, but doesn't stay that way long. Like you!"

"Another curse of being a Baldassare," Dante said.

"Or the joy of it," Cristofor replied.

Catherine stepped inside the instant Dante pulled open the door. "Why didn't you call me?" He'd obviously been asleep. His hair was mussed, his eyes not quite open. And his pajama top had been thrown on hastily. He was a patient, for heaven's sake, and she shouldn't be looking at him this way, yet this was everything sexy she remembered about Dante, and for a moment she was caught off guard.

"What the hell are you talking about?" he snapped.

"Gianni. Your father came to my cottage a little while ago. He said Gianni was sick, and needed some medicine. He asked me to come over and take a look."

Dante shook his head, then ran an impatient hand through his hair. "Gianni's fine. It's one of those childhood things…you know, they get overtired, cranky. Nothing to worry about."

Actually, she didn't know, she'd had so little experience with children. Except for a short rotation through pediatrics, she'd never worked with children at all. Even here, when a child came into rehab, she didn't take the case as they had a pediatric specialist. "He's in the waiting room, waiting for my report," she said.

"Who?"

"Your father."

"Damn it," Dante snarled. "I told him Gianni was fine, but he won't listen to me. He thinks I'm not—"

"A doctor?"

"Four years of medical school, more than that in my residency, and to my father, that means nothing." He moved aside and motioned Catherine in. "I'm sorry he dragged you into this. My father and I have a difference of opinion when it comes to the way I raise Gianni, and he shouldn't have got you involved."

"I can take a look," she offered, holding out her medical bag. "Maybe it will make him feel a little better."

"Nothing's going to make him feel better until I…" He stopped. Got married? That's what his father wanted. That's what all good sons of good Italian fathers did, wasn't it? Except he wasn't a good son in this. Not even close to being a good son. "Sure. What the hell? Take a look. Maybe he's right. Maybe I've been out of medicine too long to be a doctor."

"I doubt that, Dante. You don't lose the gift you had because you haven't used it for a while."

He smiled up at her. "Sometimes I overreact."

"Like your father does?"

Catherine slipped into the guest room and watched Gianni

sleep for a moment. He was so peaceful it was almost a shame to disturb him. Such a beautiful face...so like Dante's. She couldn't help but think that if things had gone differently for them, she might have a child who looked like this. She'd never thought much about being a mother, but when she looked down at such an angelic face, it made her heart ache. And yearn.

"He's fine," she said five minutes later. "Temperature's normal, no congestion in his lungs. He says his stomach doesn't hurt. So I think it's exactly what you said. He was a little out of sorts because he was tired."

"He's asleep again?"

Catherine nodded, a gentle smile sliding its way across her face. It was the perfect sleep of a child, she thought. "He barely woke up." Under different circumstances, she might have stayed there a while, simply watching. But the longing for what she didn't have had crept in so acutely, so unexpectedly, she had to leave before Dante saw what she was feeling. And he would.

Sighing, Catherine started for the door, but as she approached it she stopped for a moment, thought about the way she'd acted earlier, the finally turned round to face Dante. "Look, I want to apologize for this evening. It seems like I'm always apologizing to you for something, doesn't it? But I know you went to so much trouble having the dinner catered, especially with the fennel and endive. They can't be easy to find here, and I appreciate it. I was terrible company, Dante, and I'm sorry."

"You were," he said, nodding thoughtfully. "But apology accepted."

She frowned, wrinkling her nose. "We don't go well together, do we?" They should, because they had. But this time it was different. Her stomach was in knots all the time now, all over the prospect of a chance encounter in the hall, or a spur-of-the-moment meeting in the therapy room. If she dwelt on it, as she tended to do, she even got to the point where her hands shook.

"I'm sorry about that too, Dante. It's my fault. You're my patient, and as your physician I should be doing better by you, but—"

"Then you're fired," he said, his voice totally void of emotion.

In spite of his flat words, his eyes sparkled. That dark glint gave him away. Always had. "Just why would you do that *now*?" she asked, taking a step backward as he rolled a few inches forward. "Especially after I've asked several times before, and you've refused me?" She did know, actually. Which was one of the reasons for the current butterflies in her stomach. And they weren't fluttering—they were tramping.

"Because it's not professional." He moved forward again, causing her to step back enough so that her back was pressed firmly to the door.

"What's not professional? Me treating you now, with the relationship we've had in the past? Because that's what I've been saying all along, and—"

"What's not professional is what I'm about to do, Catherine. Unless you open that door and run away, what's going to happen between us should never happen between Doctor and patient. Bad medical ethics and all."

Her breath caught in her throat. This was what she'd wanted, and what she'd feared. "And what do you intend to do? Remember, Gianni's on the other side of that door." She pointed a wobbly hand in that direction, then drew it back before he could see how badly she was shaking. She'd thought about this moment. Wondered if it was inevitable. Feared it was more her own delusion than anything else. But now…she didn't know. Another fling with Dante might be pleasant for a while. For sure, she knew what she was getting. Knew every nook and cranny of it.

Of course, she'd known all that last time too, and look how that had turned out.

So, could she keep what was about to happen in its proper place? Relegate it to a casual fling and walk away unscathed when it was over? Or come away with a broken heart yet again?

Catherine drew in a pensive breath. She did know what she wanted, and what she'd do. Which was a problem. A bigger problem by far, though, was that she wasn't allowing common sense to order the situation. In fact, she was keeping it as far away from this as she could.

"I intend to do this," Dante said, as he locked the wheels of his chair and rose slowly to his feet.

She watched him stand, amazingly steady on his feet, but her gaze was not that of a Doctor watching, with rapt attention, her patient's progress. Rather, she was caught up as a lover might be, anticipating what would come next, thinking ahead to what would come after that and after that. And remembering… Dear God, how she remembered.

She wanted Dante to stop this. Right here, right now. But she couldn't find it in herself to make that demand, and there wasn't an ounce of will in her that could stop it herself, or even send her running out the door. "Dante, I…"

Finally all the way up, he laid his finger to her lips to silence her. "No words, Catherine. Not now."

But there were so many words, words that should have been spoken last time, words that had built up over the years. Words, she feared, that would only hurt her again. Yet this was Dante. "We shouldn't," she gasped, tilting her face to meet his, even though she knew she shouldn't. Perhaps even feeling a pinch of the inevitable regret that was sure to would follow.

He ran his thumb over her lips, tracing a delicate line across them then back. "You always had such soft lips," he murmured. "Soft, kissable…" Then he bent to kiss her there, a kiss even more delicate than his touch.

Catherine remembered that touch. Loved that touch. Craved it like she'd craved nothing in her life. "Dante, I don't…" Her voice trembled, not on the verge of tears but with nervousness infused with desire—a desire that was winning fast.

"You don't what?" he asked, his breath drifting warmly over

her ear as he reached behind her neck to twine her hair through his fingers. "You know how good we are. And I know what you like."

His touch caused her to shiver, and she brushed his hand away. But he was persistent, not to be dissuaded yet, pressing himself to her as he skimmed his hand underneath her sweater, only to find that she'd neglected to wear a bra for this house call. "What's this?" he asked, chuckling. "You were expecting this?"

"I was in a hurry." A lie. She had deliberately not put on her bra when she'd dressed to come and see Gianni. She'd told herself it was because she was in a hurry, and for a while she'd even believed that. But now…"Had to come see Gianni…" His hand slid up her left breast and his fingers sought her nipple. He pinched it between his thumb and forefinger, making it hard, and all the while never took his eyes off hers. Not even as she sucked in a sharp gasp, partly from the sensation, partly from the memory.

"We were good this way," he whispered, moving his fingers down her belly, tracing the line of her ribs to her waist and round to the small of her back. "You know this was always one of my favorite spots," he said, applying gentle pressure there as he kneaded with his thumbs.

Catherine fought back the moan begging to escape her. Yes, that had always been one of his favorite spots, and one of hers. And what came after…what *always* came after…. She arched into him, pushed herself against his body and raised her hands to his head, wove her fingers around his neck and entwined them in his hair. The embrace was all-encompassing. She felt the strain of his erection pressed to her belly, heard the moan catch in his throat as his fingers moved over her hip. "Dante," she whispered, not sure if that was a sign to stop, or go.

"You can still run, Catherine," he whispered, his voice raspy. "It's not too late."

"Are you sure?" she asked, sliding her hands down his back.

It was but a heartbeat later that his lips were on hers, pressing hard until his tongue was inside her mouth, flirting, stroking, then finally dominating. The kiss was so blatantly sexual, so powerful she didn't pull away. Couldn't pull away no matter what he offered.

This was the fantasy she'd dreamt for such a long time and had never thought she would have again. Yet this might be a one and only for them, the last time, the farewell they hadn't had before. An empty spot she'd buried deep inside for so long pleaded with her to make this moment linger, to give herself over to it. Which she did. Willingly.

As she continued her journey over Dante's back, he took hold of her left hand and pulled it forward, then placed a kiss in the palm. She shuddered, withdrawing her right hand and offering it up to him for the same. She fully expected he would take them both then lead her off into the suite's master bedroom, lock the door behind and…

But Dante surprised her. He placed her right hand on his heart. "It's not too late, Catherine. I'm sure of that." Then he leaned forward and kissed her gently on the lips. A kiss that was new to her. One that melted her down to her soul.

After that, he withdrew his hand, backed up, stepped away, then braced himself against the wall for support. "You were wrong, you know," he said, his voice still raspy and now a bit winded.

"About what?" she said, too confused by what had happened, *and not happened*, to make much sense of this.

"About us. We do go well together, Catherine. Very well."

She studied him for a moment, her tingling senses still not abating. "Is this some kind of a game, Dante? Did you want to get me into this position to see how far I would go? Because you know what? If it's a game, you win. I would have done it again with you. Nothing held back." Including her heart. "So you've proved yourself now. Are you happy? You're a heartbreaker, a real love 'em and leave 'em kind of guy. Nothing's changed, has it, Dante? You're still the same bastard who did this to me five years ago then cheated on me with another woman."

CHAPTER EIGHT

CATHERINE paced back and forth in tiny her office for an hour before she finally sank down onto the couch, kicked off her shoes and pretended she was going to sleep. She knew it wouldn't happen. Not after what she and Dante had just done…almost done. Would have done right there had it not been for Gianni sleeping in the next room.

What was it in her make-up that made her keep falling for him the way she did, even when she knew what it would get her? Why couldn't she resist, or simply find the will to walk away?

They'd had their rules the first time. Their relationship was supposed to have been casual and convenient. No strings, or anything that even hinted at permanence. She'd known that going in, yet it hadn't stopped her from developing feelings. Feelings that, frankly, had surprised her as the rules had been hers, not Dante's. But then he'd asked her to marry him and the rules had changed. Which had been a mistake that had changed so many other rules in life, including the one where she intended staying single because she'd said yes to him even before she'd taken a breath.

Now here she was, heading in exactly the same direction and, if anything, she needed those rules back now more than ever. Yet look at her. Willing. Able. So close. And she wasn't able to stop it. So what was it? Something in her? Or in Dante? Was it that unbelievable chemistry that came along only once in a lifetime, the chemistry that stripped away all sense and left only…vulnerability?

Or was it…?

No! She wasn't going to admit that. Not out loud. Not to herself. She'd called him a selfish bastard for walking away from her all those years ago and not giving her any choices about the way he had been willing to return, then cheating on her when she hadn't done it his way. That's where she was going to leave it now because she wasn't ready to admit that what she'd thought long since over had never stopped.

Catherine let out an exasperated sigh. Another moment or two lost in his kiss would have been too late. That's one thing she knew for sure, amid all the other uncertainties. "Stupid," she muttered, as she reached above her head to pull the chain on the light.

As the room was pitched into darkness, though, the memories she was trying to blot out flooded in even more. Dante five years ago, Dante just this evening. She desperately needed that time off she'd asked Max for. He'd said no, but now she was going to have to insist. He'd agreed if that became the case, she could go. So she would.

For the sake of her sanity.

And her heart.

That was it. The perfect solution. She'd go home for two weeks. Back to the States to visit her mother. Back to the States where she would be nowhere near Dante, and she'd have time to think. Good plan. Brilliant, in fact!

That resolve made, Catherine yanked the chain, turning the light back on, then she hopped up from the couch, padded across the carpeted floor to her desk, and turned on her computer. Her first site—one of those travel services. Three clicks later and she was looking at a whole host of airline schedules…One more click and she'd have a ticket.

She was debating the number of stops she was willing to make in her flight in order to get the best deal, her fingers poised above the mouse that would click her acceptance, when a soft knock at her door broke her attention. Dante come to apologize? Or to finish what they'd started?

She didn't say anything. Maybe he'd think she'd gone back to her house. Or was seeing a patient.

Another knock sounded, however, this one louder. Whoever was out there wasn't going away. "Come in," she finally said, bracing herself in case it was Dante. But it wasn't. It was one of the night nurses, a young woman by the name of Inga who'd been at Aeberhard only a few weeks. She was looking positively stricken about something.

"I didn't want to bother you, but…"

Catherine gestured her in further than the doorway in which she stood, clinging to the wooden frame.

"But I haven't been able to find Dr Mitthoeffer. Mrs O'Brian is having muscle spasms and I wanted him to look at her, maybe prescribe a light dose of a relaxant. But he's not answering his pager or his cellphone." Dr Johann Mitthoeffer was one of the two general surgeons employed here—he had his own surgical practice and stepped in as a part-timer for a few shifts a week. In fact, the majority of her other doctors did the same—ran their own practice elsewhere and came here for several shifts.

"Have you checked in his office?"

"Lights are out, door is locked," Inga replied.

Most odd, Catherine thought as she picked up the phone to dial Dr Mitthoeffer's cellphone. He was reliable, he didn't just wander off. None of her doctors did. But after three rings, when his phone switched to voicemail, a tiny chill wiggled up her back. Mitthoeffer didn't know she was in the building tonight so, as far as he was concerned, he was the only Doctor actually in the clinic.

Yet he wasn't answering!

Catherine stood, grabbed a set of pass keys from her desk, pulled on her white jacket and headed for the door, slipping into her shoes on the way. Two minutes later she was entering Dr Mitthoeffer's office. "Perhaps he left a note," she said to Inga, who was right on her heels. She hoped so as with any other scenario, she was afraid she'd have to relieve him of his duty here. Which she didn't want to do. While they rarely had an occasion to use Dr Mitthoeffer as a surgeon, it was always good to know he was on staff and available as he was an excellent doctor.

Two steps into the office Catherine turned on the light. Immediately, she discovered Mitthoeffer's tan wool coat hanging on the coat tree. Next to it sat the boots he wore for trudging through the snow.

So he was here.

The warning hairs on the back of her neck shot up, and Catherine practically ran to Dr Mitthoeffer's desk where, behind it, she found him sprawled in a heap on the floor. His face was the whitish-gray shade of death, causing her to fear the worst as she dropped to her knees next to him, immediately searching for a pulse. Thank God it was there. Faint, thready, but definitely there. "Call a code," she instructed Inga. Normally a code blue was reserved for a resuscitation and, technically, Dr Mitthoeffer didn't need that as he had a pulse and he was dragging in tiny gulps of air. But she needed what was available on the crash cart—a cart chock full of emergency medical supplies.

"Johann, can you hear me?" she called, pulling the penlight from her pocket to assess his pupillary action. Sluggish, not following the light.

Stroke?

"Johann, listen to me!"

At first, she wasn't sure he could hear, but after a long moment he did stir a little, attempting to raise his right index finger. He didn't open his eyes, though.

"Look, Johann, I need you to tell me what happened, if you can." A heart attack was a strong possibility, too, and she was beginning to rule out a stroke as he was moving both his arms reflexively now. "Good, Johann," she said, grabbing her stethoscope from her pocket, sticking in her earpieces and taking a listen to his chest. Seemed normal enough. Heart ticking away, too fast, too faint, but fighting to keep going.

It wasn't acting like a heart attack either as he was burning up with fever. Even without a thermometer, she could feel the heat rolling off his body. Infection of some sort? "Have you been ill?" she asked, beginning a rapid assessment, starting at his neck. She felt for swelling, abnormalities, and finding none moved on down. "Or allergic to anything?" This could be an anaphylactic reaction of some sort, but she didn't think so.

His eyes fluttered open briefly. Normally a robust man of fifty, right now Johann Mitthoeffer looked twenty years older than that as he struggled to focus on her. He opened his mouth to speak, but nothing came out. His hand fluttered away from his side, though, and he pointed weakly to his right lower abdomen.

Appendicitis? Most people felt the pain of it, but in some rare instances that wasn't the case. Occasionally it manifested as only a twinge, or there were no symptoms at all. Was that what was happening here? "Your appendix?" she asked, shifting her position at his side.

He blinked, rather than nodding.

"I think it's ruptured, Johann." That made sense. Ruptured appendix, infection. Elevated temperature. Critical illness. She was fairly certain now that the infected appendix had burst, spread its poisons, and Johann had probably been close to dying even before he'd known he was ill.

He blinked again, shuddered out a ragged sigh when she gently prodded his right lower abdomen, and faded back into unconsciousness.

"Dr Wilder?" Inga called, pushing the crash cart in through the office door.

"Oxygen first," Catherine said, rising up on her knees to look over Johann's desk. "Get his blood pressure reading, then start an IV. Also…call Dr…No, I'll do that."

She pushed herself up off the floor, made way for Inga to get through, then instructed the other nurse who'd followed her in to go and prepare the operating theater for surgery. Yes, they did have a small one there. Rarely used, and not set up for anything major. She'd rather have sent Johann to the city—bigger facilities, more doctors—but the trip would kill him, if the poison surging through his body didn't get him first.

Another of the nurses came in—the director of the night shift. Marie Ober was a stout woman, very no-nonsense, and once she was on the scene Catherine trusted her to make sure everything was done properly. "Get his vitals, then get him ready to transport to surgery. I've got to go call Dr Rand and get him in here as fast as I can," she said, on her way out the door. Dr Rand was the second of their surgeons.

Such good staff, Catherine thought as she ran back to her office to look up Dr Eric Rand's telephone number. Thank God, he lived only a few short kilometers from the clinic. Otherwise… well, she didn't want to think about that.

Catherine flipped though her card file and rang up Eric as quickly as her fingers could punch in the numbers. After three rings, his wife answered. "Eric's not here tonight," she informed Catherine. "He's gone to Paris for the next two days, a medical seminar. Since he wasn't on your surgical schedule, neither was he on call…" The rest of the words were a blur, and when Catherine hung up, her mind was already racing ahead to another plan. Maybe Dr Franz? He was retired from surgery now, and lived some way out, but he could be here in less than two hours. Or Dr Dowd? He wasn't a surgeon, but he'd gone through part of a surgical residency before switching to sports medicine. And he was just an hour away.

Not good choices, she thought as her mind went to Dante. He could do it. For him, it would be easy even after all this time. She'd seen that before with Mrs Gunter. Dante's surgical skills were still polished, still perfect.

But would he do it? Resuscitating a woman from anaphylactic shock the way he had done was a simple thing, but this was a life-threatening condition.

And *Dr* Dante Baldassare was her only hope because this was a procedure she could not work her way through the way she could have with Mrs Gunter's tracheotomy. This required precise surgical skill, and she wasn't a surgeon.

There wasn't time to think, wasn't time to debate the choices. Johann was hovering so close to death there wasn't a minute to waste.

Quickly she rang up Max, explained the situation, and asked him to come in and take call, as she expected to assist in surgery. Then she ran down the hall to Dante's suite and pounded on the door. When he didn't answer immediately, she went in. "Dante!" she shouted, flipping on the overhead light in the entry vestibule then rushing into his bedroom.

"What the hell?" he shouted.

"I have a patient with a ruptured appendix. Don't have a surgeon here, can't get one in time, and can't get Johann out in time to save his life."

"And you expect me to do what?" Slowly, he swung his legs over the side of the bed, but made no attempt to get up.

"Operate."

He shook his head. "No," he said, his voice dead serious. "I can't do that."

"You're the only one who can."

"But I can't. Do you know how long it's been?"

"Then he'll die," she said, not even trying to soften the impact of her words. "Dr Johann Mitthoeffer, our surgeon, is unconscious, his appendix has ruptured, and right now infection is spreading though his body. His vital signs are weak, he's barely hanging on, and we have no other options. Either you do it, or I'll have to take a try at it myself." A thought that horrified her as she was wholly unqualified. But there was nothing else.

"You can't operate, Catherine. If it's ruptured, and the infection is already spreading..." Dante gave his head an impatient shake. "You'll kill him if you don't know what you're doing."

"He's going to die anyway."

"Do you have someone for anesthesia?"

"My chief nurse was a nurse anesthetist. She's already prepping."

"And a scrub tech?"

"Inga will do."

Forcing out an angry sigh, he rose to his feet. "Have someone call my father or Cristofor to come stay with Gianni. The number for their hotel is in the medical chart."

Catherine blinked her surprise. "You'll do it?"

"I sure as hell don't want to. I haven't held a scalpel in five years except in those few minutes with your peanut allergy patient, and you're giving me a patient who probably won't make it. It's not a good situation, Catherine, and I hate like hell that you're dragging me into it. But, yes, I'll do it but only because you don't give me another choice." He pointed to the wheelchair at the side of the room. "Take me down in that. It'll be faster." Then he threw on a robe and dropped down into the chair, and they were off, not a word spoken between them until they reached the operating theater.

"Your father is on his way," Inga told Dante, as Catherine wheeled him into the prep room. "I've assigned one of the nurse aides to stay with your son until your father arrives."

Dante managed a pleasant smile for Inga. "I appreciate that," he said, then pushed himself to the edge of the wheelchair, and stood. "Now," he said, turning towards Catherine as Inga scurried from the room, "I need surgical scrubs, shoe covers and whatever the hell they use as protective gear in surgery these days."

He was in a snit. She didn't blame him. Under the same circumstances she would have been, too. In a snit, or worse. And as she watched him pull off his silk pajamas and slip into surgical scrubs, paying no heed to the fact that he was quite naked underneath or that she was watching, and as he limped his way over to the surgical supply shelf for protective eyewear, it hit her. That admission she didn't want to say aloud, or even think. An admission that was pounding at her. *She loved Dante*. Was in love with him. The real kind of love. The kind that hadn't died over all these years.

She'd never, ever been just a little in love with him, as she'd tried to convince herself she was. In fact, she'd never loved him as much as she did right now.

She'd never tell him, of course. Couldn't tell him. His life scared her. And he scared her for all the things he was, and wasn't. But the man she was watching at this moment was the man she'd always known he was…the one she'd fallen in love with years ago, when she'd been too stupid to realize that it had been more than a crush or a reaction to their chemistry.

Catherine wasn't sure that this startling revelation meant anything in terms of her own life, because she still couldn't have Dante. But the little tangle of apprehension that had been sitting in the pit of her stomach since he'd come to Aeberhard had just shrunk. Knowing for sure what she felt was bad. But it was good, too. "Thank you," she whispered, as he pulled on a surgical cap. "Thank you for doing this."

He gave her an odd look, and his eyes softened. "It scares the hell out of me, Catherine. I shouldn't be going anywhere near that patient, and I'm not ashamed to admit it. If the man wasn't about to die, I wouldn't."

She smiled sympathetically. "You'll save him, Dante. You're a brilliant surgeon."

"In the past. A long time ago."

"Maybe. But I don't believe you've forgotten it, or lost your skills," she said softly. Walking over to Dante, she stopped in front of him, leaned up and kissed him lightly on the lips. "I don't believe that at all."

Turning to the sink to commence scrubbing, he tapped the foot pedal to let the water flow, then dipped his arms into the spray. "You'll be there?"

"Right across the table from you."

He turned and studied her face for a moment, as she studied his. From that point on they didn't say another word to each other. Not as they scrubbed, not as they finished dressing, pulled up masks and walked into the operating theater.

Not until she was standing across the operating table from him, and he was calling for a scalpel.

If he'd thought the pain after his accident had been the worst thing he'd ever experienced, he'd been wrong. This was the worst pain. Right now! His legs burned so badly he couldn't move them. His hands ached from the tension of gripping the scalpel so tightly he'd actually cut off circulation in his fingers twice during the three-hour procedure. And there were no words to describe what was going on in his neck and back.

He was so out of shape. How had he ever done this before?

Honestly, he couldn't remember. He'd been in top condition back when he had been a surgeon, but overall he was in much better physical shape now. His body was toned in only the way an athlete would be. He worked out and exercised daily because races were an event of endurance. They were long, hard, fast. A human body had to be ready for the competition, had to be ready for the pounding that went on for hours. Yet a human body also had to be ready to do what he'd done, and his body was not. Thank God Hans had heard news of what was happening and had come into the clinic. For the last hour and a half he'd literally acted as a prop to Dante, letting Dante shift his weight to Hans when he'd needed to. Then afterwards, when the surgery had ended, and Catherine had been closing the incision, finishing the other last details, Hans had been the one to help him into the wheelchair, then brought him here to the whirlpool.

Aeberhard had a good staff. Dedicated beyond the call of duty. Word of the crisis had spread quickly and, according to Catherine, most of the staff had wandered in, without being asked, to see if they could be of help. She was lucky to be working in such a place, and in many respects he was sure that the quality of the staff reflected the quality of its director. Catherine was extraordinary. She'd proved that tonight, staying with him throughout the surgery, assisting in everything he asked, even though her surgical experience could have been measured in a thimble.

He admired her…as a person, as a physician. Something he wished he'd done all those years ago. He also wished he hadn't taken her so for granted. That, perhaps, had been the worst mistake he'd ever made.

"You decent?" she asked, stepping into the therapy room.

Hans had gone to catch up on some overdue paperwork, leaving Dante alone in the warm water, at Dante's request. After the surgery, he hadn't been in the mood to be around other people. Still wasn't. Except for Catherine. "Depends on what you mean by decent," he said, his voice sounding so weary, even to his ears.

"Well, I came by to tell you that your dad took Gianni back to the hotel. He thought that you might want to sleep for a while before you have to deal with him."

Dante sighed. "Gianni doesn't even know I'm a doctor."

"You've never told him?"

"Never been a reason to. In his world, I drive a race car. That's enough." He shifted in the water, then yawned. "He's heard my father say too many bad things about doctors…"

"Because of Dario?"

Dante nodded. "My father blamed the doctors for his death. Initially, they told him the prognosis was good. But he'd suffered a little rip in his aorta. Something they didn't catch right away."

"And he bled to death?" she gasped.

"As a result, my father will ridicule a doctor every chance he gets. He's bitter, and hurt. And I think me being a doctor reminds him. So we don't talk about it."

"I'm so sorry. That must be tough. Not just your brother's death, but the rift in your family."

"Sometimes avoiding the obvious is the easiest thing to do."

"And sometimes it's not. Sometimes it hurts so bad." She turned away and walked over to the window, where she pulled back the blinds to look outside.

He saw the pain in her eyes and wanted to ask more, but he knew this side of Catherine, the side that was locked up emotionally. She dealt with the bad things in her life by walking away, just like she was doing now, even if the walk was only to the other side of the room. "Do you want to tell me?" he asked gently.

"Tell you what?"

"What really hurt you? Was it truly me, Catherine?"

"Don't give yourself so much credit, Dante. You only had six months of my life. The impact wasn't that great. We had a short-lived, superficial engagement neither of us was ready for. We both knew that."

Yet she sounded so hurt. So sad. Hearing her voice, how could he believe her words? "Catherine, I…"

"There's nothing to talk about, Dante. No deep, dark secrets to reveal. No admissions that when I kicked you out of my life, it ruined me, because it didn't. I'm just fine. Always have been."

Dante leaned his head back against the side of the whirlpool and shut his eyes. Her wall was up now, stronger than ever. Catherine wasn't going to talk about herself, and that was that. The window had opened a crack, then slammed shut. "And you love what you do," he said, almost sarcastically. "Love your life. Everything is just fine."

"Yes. Just fine."

Then why did her voice sound so sad?

"Would you ever go back to medicine, Dante? I know we've talked about this before, but if you don't recover enough to race again, would you return to medicine?"

This was Catherine avoiding the subject again. Apparently, avoiding the obvious was the easiest thing for her to do, too. Better that than making her sad again. "I've thought about that. Sometimes I think I might, but I'm not ready to leave racing. I've got good driving years ahead of me yet, I hope, and after that, maybe team management. It doesn't make any sense to live in a dream world, and for me that's what medicine has become. A dream that doesn't have a place in my life."

"And you can't find a place for it?"

"Doing what, Catherine? Rushing into surgery on call, as you've had me do? It doesn't work that way. I've been good in a pinch, but I can't run back and forth from one life to another and, so far I haven't found a way to make all my lives fit together."

"So your choice is set in stone." Statement, not question.

"Stone."

She finally turned to face him. "Then it's a pity, Dante, because I stood across the table from you, saw the passion in your eyes. You love it. Love it as much as you do racing, I'd guess."

"Like I said before, we don't always get what we want." And being in the same room with Catherine, so close to everything he wanted, and yet so far away from it, was proof of that. She hated his racing and that wasn't going to change. He knew that. She wanted him to be a doctor again, but he couldn't, and that wasn't going to change, either.

"I've just spent three hours standing across the table from a brilliant doctor. You saved Johann's life, Dante. Doesn't that mean anything to you?"

"Of course it does. But that doesn't change things. I gave up medicine five years ago, and I haven't taken it back based on one surgery. That's not my life any more, Catherine. I have a passion for surgery but I also have a passion for driving. I know you find it difficult to accept, but that's what I want to do." And so the argument started again. It seemed that it couldn't be avoided. That's what they did best these days.

Wearily, Dante grabbed the towel off the side of the whirlpool, wrapped it around himself and stood up, wobbling a bit as he did so. Catherine rushed forward to grab his arm to steady him, but he pushed her away. So she walked away, left him standing there with a towel wrapped around his waist as Hans came in to help him. And he watched her, too tired to argue, too tired to call her back. There was so much on his mind tonight—Catherine, Gianni. How much he missed his brother. How, if he'd been there that day, he would have stopped Dario from driving. But he hadn't been there, and Dario had died.

Why the hell did he let down everybody he loved?

CHAPTER NINE

"You *look* awfully worried," Max said sympathetically. He handed a mug of steaming hot tea across the desk to Catherine, then sat down across from her, holding his own cup of tea. "Tea and sympathy is always a nice cure," he said, settling in. "If you want it."

Catherine smiled half-heartedly, then took a sip, enjoying the warmth of the liquid as it trickled down her throat. Once it had settled in her belly, she sighed. "I'm tired. That's all it is. And…" She paused for a moment, contemplating her next words. Perhaps saying them out loud would help. And Max did have a right to know. Besides, he had such a compassionate shoulder, and so much wisdom, both of which she desperately needed right now. "And being here with Dante. I was about to book a reservation to go home for a while when all this with Johann came up." She held up a hand to stop him from saying the obvious words. "I know. I was running away. You don't have to point that out."

"If you need to go that badly, then, by all means, go, my dear. If it's something you need to settle your life, we can manage here without your for a little while. But only for a little while."

Catherine shook her head. "I'm not going. Not with Johann sick now. We don't have another doctor to replace him."

"Is it the work that's getting to you, or is it a private matter with Dante? Or am I being too personal, asking?"

"I thought I was over him, Max," she said. "We were involved for a while, not very long, but it's been years. I've been married once since that, for heaven's sake! And yet here he is, and I've been a total mess since he arrived."

"In love?"

Catherine shrugged, even though she knew.

"Well, perhaps this is something you should be telling him. Words to whisper in his ear rather than mine." He chuckled. "Whispering the right words in the right ear can be as good for you as tea and sympathy. Better!"

"Or they can further prove how pathetic I am."

"Falling in love isn't pathetic. I've always thought it was wonderful. Rather wished I'd had time to do it more often." Max laughed. "It does make you crazy, though, but it's a good kind of crazy. We should all be so lucky as to be in love a time or two in our lives."

"That depends on what you mean by good," she said despondently. Sliding down into her chair, she took another sip of tea and felt the relaxing effect seeping in all the way to her toes. "And I think the feeling is totally underrated."

"Underrated because he doesn't know how you feel about him, and not knowing usually means unrequited. Is that it? Your feelings are unrequited?"

"No, that's not the problem. They are requited. But what good would it do, telling him how I feel when we're so wrong for each other?"

"Well, my dear, that's something for you to figure out on your own." He scooted to the edge of his chair, then stood to leave. "Or not."

Catherine studied Max for a moment as he walked to the door. Many things needed figuring out, didn't they? Dante held a piece of her life in the palm of his hand, yet so did Max. "It's time, Max," she said, as he reached for the doorknob.

"For what?" he said, without turning around.

"For you to tell me *why me*? That's something I've been trying to figure out for over a year now, and you've put me off every time I've asked. It involves me and I don't want to be left out again. Either you tell me what I want to know, or I'll leave for good."

He arched his eyebrows. "That's harsh, don't you think?"

"So is making a decision that includes me without including me. I can't do that any more. And I can't let you do that to me, either. So, tell me, Max. Tell me right now or you'll have my resignation within the hour."

"Then it seems you're ready. I've wondered when that would happen."

Perhaps she was. Perhaps she was ready for more than Max's explanation. She drew in a slow, deep breath then let it out reluctantly. "Yes, I'm ready. Tell me why you chose me. I hadn't practiced medicine too many years when you sought me out, I'd had no admin experience at all, and you did have several doctors here already who could have stepped into the job. But you came after me specifically, and don't tell me it had anything to do with our brief meeting in Boston all those years ago when I sneaked into your lecture and we shared dinner afterwards, because that's not it."

Max drew in a ragged breath, and turned slowly to face her. "That meeting in Boston after my lecture was planned. I meant to look you up, Catherine. That wasn't the reason for my trip there but it was at the top of my list of things I wanted to do once I'd arrived." He paused, and Catherine didn't know if he was putting her off once more or trying to find the right words.

She watched him walk to the window, pull back the blinds and stare outside for a full minute. He squared his shoulders, and she wondered what made this so difficult for him. "I do have a right to know," she said gently, but more to remind herself than him.

Max nodded his head. "That you do, but it's not so easy for me because I know how difficult your relationship with Emil Brannon was."

"My father?" she asked, too stunned to think ahead to what her father had to do with this.

"Your father. I know how he turned his back on his family to pursue other interests, and how much that hurt you. I've been afraid that telling you what I have to would cause you more pain, and I've never wanted to do that, Catherine."

"I wasn't aware I'd said that much to you about him." It was something she kept to herself. One of those deeply hurtful parts of her life that could never be resolved now that her father was dead. One of those matters best left buried with him.

"You haven't said that much to me, Catherine But Emil did. Many times over the years. Every time you two fought, every time he pushed you away, or you pushed him away, I heard about it."

Catherine blinked, trying to absorb what Max was saying. "You…you knew my father?"

He nodded, but said nothing.

"Tell me, Max," she cried. "Tell me how you knew him!"

He finally turned around, and a sad smile turned down the corners of his lips. "I wasn't always such an old, out-of-shape man, the way you see me now. Once I was quite fit. I liked to ski, to climb. I liked to take a few risks, the way Emil did. We lived similar lives, had similar fascinations."

Catherine sucked in a sharp breath. She hadn't expected this from Max. He was the man who fixed the broken bodies of those who lived the way her father had. He was the stability she'd never found anywhere else. That's the only thing that made sense to her.

"I was going up Everest. Small expedition, very knowledgeable Sherpa to guide us. Met your father there. Halfway up we ran into bad weather. I didn't want to turn back, neither did he, so we didn't." He drew in a ragged breath. "We thought we'd walk through the weather, or dig in and wait it out. It was bad, not horrible. So we made camp…there were five of us left at that point. And we waited."

She'd never heard this story. Of course, she'd heard very few of her father's stories. He'd never let her get that close to him, never let her into his life.

"After a couple of days the weather seemed to be letting up, so we decided to commence our climb again. But the weather was deceptive...a small break didn't mean it was getting better. We walked into a total white-out, the wind so bitter and cold we couldn't breathe, the chill so harsh it froze us. We knew it was time to go, to get off the mountain if we could. But we couldn't. Three of our party died up there, unfortunately. They were lost...buried somewhere in the snow where we couldn't find them and left there in a frozen grave for eternity. Emil was injured...frostbite, disorientation, lack of oxygen. I wasn't quite so bad, but I was suffering." He glanced down at his feet and winced. "Lost one toe on my right foot and two on my left at the end of it all."

His slight limp! Now she understood.

"I can't even begin to describe what it's like being up there, knowing you're going to die. At first you're afraid. You fight it. You pray to God to save you. But eventually death becomes part of your reality. The fear goes away and you think death will come as a relief. Finally, you pray for it to come quickly and merci-fully. All those hours...days...while Emil and I huddled together, praying alternately to be saved and to die, he talked about you. Even when he was out of his head. You were quite the young lady...so talented. We looked at the picture of you that he carried...handled it so much we wore it out in a short time." He lifted his gaze to Catherine. "Emil loved you, Catherine. You were his passion and his greatest pride."

"Then why didn't he stop? After his Everest climb, after he'd been so close to death, why didn't he stop? We wanted him to. My mother and I begged..." With the back of her hand Catherine swiped angrily at the tears spilling down her cheeks. "Why didn't he love me enough to come home and be my father?"

"He loved you to distraction, but you can't change the nature of a man, my dear. Your father was who he had to be, and I can't offer you another explanation. I don't think he always liked what he did, I know he despised himself for always putting his family second, but I don't think he could control it."

"But you stopped, Max. Didn't you stop?"

He shrugged. "Because I was who I had to be…a doctor. That was always first in my life, and it was a promise I made to myself when we were up there. That if we got back, I would do what I was meant to do. "

"Up on Everest, how did you get back?"

"The weather did let up a bit. Emil was unconscious by then, or at least lapsing in and out. Physically, I was doing a little better than he was. We'd been huddled together in our tent for days, dying inch by inch, and I decided that I'd give it one last go. Either get us both off the mountain or end the ordeal." He shuddered. "You see bodies up there. Those left behind and frozen. But I was a doctor and I couldn't leave Emil there. That went against who I was, so…"

"You carried him down," she said in a hoarse whisper. "You carried my father off the mountain. I remember my father speaking of the doctor who'd carried him down from a mountain, but that's all I ever knew. He would tell the story in whispers to his friends, tell it when he thought I wasn't listening."

Max nodded. "Like I said, we have to be true to who we are. I couldn't have done anything else. And afterwards…your father was grateful. The money to start this clinic came from his pocket, not mine. It's one of the things we talked about when we were up there…regrets for the things we hadn't done. Mine was this clinic. It was always my dream, but I was never able to afford it when I was younger."

"Did he have any regrets?" she asked tentatively.

"Many," Max said. "And all were about his family. He regretted not being a better husband, regretted not being a better father.

Regretted the compulsion in him that split him apart from his family. Regretted that he could not overcome it. Most of all, though, he regretted missing your life. But he said that with the way he lived, he always knew death was a possibility, so he stayed away from you, pushed you away so that wouldn't touch you so badly if he did die. He always said he didn't want to spoil the one perfect thing in his life with the way he lived his life."

"He stayed away from me to protect me?" she cried. "Because he loved me?"

Max nodded.

"How could he, Max? All I ever wanted was to be important to him. All I ever wanted was to know that he loved me."

"You were important, Catherine. But he knew he was a man obsessed by something that could hurt you deeply."

"I'm not a weak person," Catherine said.

"No, you're not. But Emil always saw you as someone he had to protect. The way a father protects a child. That was the only way he knew to be your father."

"Yet he wouldn't tell me. And he let me lash out at him so many times, push him away, tell him I hated him." She was quiet for a few moments, too numb to think, to hurt to make full sense of what she was hearing. "Because he loved me?"

"Because he loved you."

So much remorse, so much regret…so much pain, when a few simple words could have healed so much. She couldn't think about it, couldn't make sense yet of how her father had twisted her life in so many ways…ways that had hurt everyone. All these years of feeling so…so alone, so rejected. Years that could have been cured with a few simple words. *Daddy*, she thought. *How could you*?

Because he'd loved her. Max wouldn't lie about that. Her father had loved her and while that didn't make her feel any better now, in time she hoped it would. "He lent you the money for the clinic," she finally said, because there was nothing else to say, nothing that could make right all the wrong.

Max shook his head. "Not lent. He gave me the money. He wanted his life to stand for something permanent. Something meaningful."

"And I wasn't?"

"You were, Catherine, but I think it's going to take a while for you to know that in your heart, for you to fully understand why Emil did what he did. He broke your heart, but his heart was broken, too."

If her father hadn't been able to say these things to her, why had her mother not said them? Why on earth had her mother not spoken of the things Max was now speaking of? Had her hurt run so deeply, too? Had her mother been shut out the way she had been, as a way to protect her from what her own husband had thought was inevitable? Then she, in turn, had shut out her daughter because that's all she knew how to do? "They wouldn't let me be included, Max. I lived on the outside always looking in."

"Because they didn't know how to do it differently. Parents aren't perfect people, Catherine. They can make horrendous mistakes, even if for the right reasons."

Catherine's tears had stopped for a moment, but now they were flowing again. "This was my father's clinic, so why didn't you name it after him?"

"In my heart, yes, it was his clinic. He refused to have his name on it, though, because he was a humble man. A truly humble man. And he wanted no interest in the clinic in any material way. But Emil did make this clinic possible, and after I learned that you were going to be a rehabilitation specialist, I knew I wanted you here. It seemed fitting."

"Yet you refused to tell me why."

"Because you weren't ready. I know you loved your father, Catherine. But you also have so much bitterness in your heart for him, and I didn't think you were ready for the truth. You might not have come here, or stayed. You had to learn to love this place, and find the passion for it that I have. Now, though, you're on the verge of the same conflicts you had with your father, but for another man you love. To resolve one is to resolve the other."

"You made the decision for me!" she cried bitterly. "Don't you understand? All this time when I wanted to know…"

"But did you, Catherine? Did you really want to know? Because you always stepped back when I refused to tell you and accepted my decision. You never demanded to know. And with Emil, did you ever demand to know why he pushed you away, or was it easier to accept that without a fight, too?"

"That's not fair," she cried. "You weren't there. You didn't know."

"What I know is that it's often easier to acquiesce. If we do that, if we let them have their way, maybe they'll love us more. You're a gentle soul, Catherine. You know how to fight for your patients, but you've never known how to fight for yourself. And, yes, that's your father's fault. You tried too hard to be the good little girl he would love, but you were fighting against a man who had his own demons to deal with."

"When I begged my father, he always said I was breaking his heart…"

"So you quit begging. Quit asking. Quit imposing yourself. You just stepped back and let it happen. It became a habit, my dear. To get people to like you…"

Catherine shuddered, and wrapped her arms protectively around herself. What Max was saying was true. She saw that now. "Begging and asking didn't work. My father never gave up his lifestyle, not even after he almost died. So everything I wanted, every time I begged…all empty words. How can I resolve that, Max?" she cried, her tears now turning to sobs. "How can I resolve that in my father, or even in Dante? He's just like my father. Shouldn't love be enough to make either of them quit doing the things that shut out the people they love?"

"Shouldn't love be enough to support them if they don't? The best life isn't measured in quantity, Catherine, but in quality. Your father suffered for what he lost, as I suspect your Dante does. It broke Emil's heart in the end, because he knew he'd lost you, knew he'd pushed you too far away."

"And it broke our hearts," she whispered. "My mother's and mine." She swiped at the tears again, then looked up at Max. "Did you make a promise to my father to bring me here to work? Is that why you asked me to take over here, and why you're giving me part-ownership? Because you feel obligated to him?"

Max shook his head. "I asked you here because you are so much like your father. He was a strong, wise man, and a man filled with much compassion. More than anything, though, he had such a passion for life. I saw that in you the first time we met. I saw Emil in you, and that's when I knew you had to be the one. My wife left me when I was young...left me because she couldn't abide my lifestyle then, all the risks I took. So I had no children, no son or daughter to go to medical school and take over here for me. But that time up on Everest, when Emil talked about you, and we looked at your picture...he was so proud that you wanted to go to medical school, to become a doctor. He told me that it would vindicate his worthless life."

"But he didn't lead a worthless life," she cried.

"For him, failing at the things that mattered most to him made his life worthless. You and your mother mattered most but he wouldn't allow you to get close enough to know that."

"You were right," Catherine whispered, pulling open her desk drawer and grabbing a box of tissues. "I wasn't ready for this before...not sure I'm ready now." So many things about her father she'd never known...never understood.

"Everything in its own good time, Catherine. You had to demand this from me. You had to make it your choice and not mine. You're such a fighter, but never for yourself, for what you want. I think the term is tender-hearted."

"Or cowardly." She did run away, figuratively speaking. It was easier, and blaming her parents convenient. Blaming her ex-husband, blaming Dante…"Maybe I'm just a coward."

"Not a coward. Just someone who grew up in a tough situation and coped the only way she knew how. But I've watched you this past year, watched you make this clinic your own, and I know you love it now. And nobody here pushes you around, Catherine. You've learned to be in charge of what you want." Max ambled to the door, then paused before stepping into the hall. "And for what it's worth, you've truly grown into the position here. Initially, I wanted you because you were your father's daughter, but I've kept you and offered you part-ownership because you are who you are. You always make the right decisions and there's no doubt who's in charge. Now it's time to do the same in your personal life."

If there was one word that could have adequately described how she was feeling, it was *numb*. Six hours after Max had told her about her father, and pointed out her rather dismaying character flaw she'd have preferred not being forced into thinking about, she still wasn't able to feel anything. She'd bundled up, trudged across the compound to her little house, then huddled under a blanket in front of the fireplace, brooding. The fire had long since burnt down to embers and a chill had filled the room, but she didn't care. Getting up and adding more logs required an effort she simply couldn't make right now. The funny thing was, she couldn't even think, either. She wanted to think about her father, try and put some sense to the things she'd never known about him. Things she'd never admitted about herself. But she was blotting him out. Blotting out everything. Just knowing that he'd loved her, and how his heart had been broken for it, stopped her from thinking beyond that. If only she'd known all this before he'd died.

She couldn't think about Dante, either. Somehow her mind wasn't processing the difficult situations in her life, the ones thrust upon her, the ones she'd created herself. They were there, but not in a seamless form right now. More like bits and pieces floating around, pinging her with little notions that made no sense.

She'd actually dialed her mother's phone number hours ago, thinking that they should talk. But she'd hung up after the second ring. This wasn't the time. She wasn't ready. And it was something best done in person.

So she'd watched the fire burn down, going from flame to a flicker, and deliberately filled her mind with work matters, the inconsequential things that took up space in her thoughts—purchase orders, work schedules. She'd forced her concentration on these things until they'd dwindled to the point that she was merely watching the fire, thinking nothing. That, right then, was a good thing as the weather outside was turning bad, and she didn't want to think about how it had turned bad on her father that day up on Everest. Or how it had turned bad that day when Dante had crashed. A horrendous snowstorm for her father, a simple light rain for Dante. Bad results. Shutting out the emotions and the people she shouldn't have shut out—even worse results.

As the flames died to sparks, however, and the numbness inside her died down with it, all she had left were thoughts about the things she didn't want to think about yet. So she forced herself out of her stupor, threw off her blanket, and trudged back outside and across to the clinic.

At the door to Aeberhard, she paused for a moment, looking up at the sky. It was a beautiful night, really. Snowing, but in a peaceful way. It reminded her of words from the old Christmas hymn…*"All is calm, all is bright."*

If only she could find that same peace in her soul. That same calmness. That same brightness.

* * *

Dante closed the children's book and laid it aside. Gianni was asleep now, curled up in the bed right next to him. He would be going home tomorrow, back to Tuscany, and already Dante missed him. But in another week or so, he'd be going home, too. He looked forward to that. Looked forward to stepping back into his life. But he also dreaded it, because he knew Catherine would never be part of that life. The space between them was too great and, no matter what his feelings for her, he didn't see how anything could change.

In the end, he was still a race driver, and she'd never accept that. It frightened her and that wouldn't change. To be true to himself meant to be without Catherine, and to have Catherine meant he couldn't be true to himself. This was the race he could not win and, to be honest, there wasn't even any point lining up at the starting line.

Dante stretched out alongside Gianni, reflecting on the amazing ways his life had changed, having this child with him now. Dario's gift to him, and the reason he'd come to understand the true nature of his soul. He'd always loved Gianni, at first as a nephew and now as a son. The responsibility of raising him had scared him to death at the start, and still did sometimes. But they were growing up together, as well as growing together. Just the two of them…Sometimes, though, when he closed his eyes, the two of them turned into three. A perfect image, and another piece of his soul. If only he knew how to get through to Catherine.

But Catherine didn't want to be reached, or touched. So, no matter what he felt, it didn't matter.

Sighing, Dante pulled Gianni into his arms and held him close. The boy needed to go off to his own bed to sleep, but not for a few more minutes.

The following morning the snow was coming down harder, and Catherine was glad to be safe and warm inside. She needed that security right now, when so many other things in her life were turning upside down. The interaction between Gianni and Dante, which she was watching through the glass in the door, was amazing. Dante was a natural with the boy, and the boy responded as any boy would with his father.

The way she would have responded to her father had he let her.

Dante and Gianni had been swimming for several minutes already, Dante as part of his physical therapy and Gianni for the fun of it. That's one of the things she dearly loved about Aeberhard—the traditional medical and therapy lines were not drawn too hard. Where was it written that physical therapy had to be rigorous exercise, and where was it written that physical therapy could not be playtime in a swimming pool between father and son, like she was watching?

Dante was getting better and stronger every day. The function in his ankle was improving, the range of motion much improved. He did still have some residual weakness after long periods of time on his feet or strenuous exercise, but even that was steadily improving. Although she was no longer his physician—that duty had been turned over to Friedrich Rilke now, in the best interests of all involved— she did still keep a close watch on his progress as she did with all the patients here. Another week and Dante would be ready to leave.

A lump formed in Catherine's throat as she peeked through the window at them. Even in her brief marriage she'd never wanted the coziness of a relationship like she was seeing now. Hadn't wanted it, hadn't planned it. *Pulled away from it*. She wasn't sure what she'd planned on happening after the wedding vows. "Because Robert wasn't you," she said sadly, watching Dante climb out of the pool. She'd only loved Dante. She knew that now. More, she would never love anyone else that way.

She was at her desk an hour later when a tiny knock at the door barely caught her attention.

"I came to say goodbye," Gianni said from the doorway, not

coming fully into her office. "My grandpa and Uncle Cristofor are taking me back home now, so my papa can rest more."

"Does your father know you're here?" she asked.

Gianni shook his head. "He's talking to my grandfather about race things. But I know my way around here now. I won't get lost this time. Your hospital is very small."

Brave child. He knew what he wanted and went after it. She admired that, especially in someone so young. Things could have been so different for her if she'd been more like Gianni, or her father had been like Dante, who included his child no matter what he had to do, who he had to fight. "Do you know your way to the kitchen?" she asked.

Gianni nodded. "Greta, the cook, gives me biscuits when I stop there."

"Want to stop off there now?" she asked. "I could use a fresh biscuit myself." Catherine stood, walked around her desk, then held out her hand to Gianni. "Then we'd better get back to your father's suite before he misses you."

"You can sneak me in again," Gianni said, grinning up shyly at her. "My papa won't see me."

A child who knew what he wanted *and* wasn't afraid to say so. Dante was, indeed, doing a very good job even with a difficult life. He was everything a father should be.

Dante waved goodbye one more time as the car drove through the Aeberhard gates. In another week they'd be back together again. But that seemed so long.

For a moment, during his last hug from Gianni, he'd thought about calling it quits here and going with them. He'd made good progress and surely he could find another therapist in Tuscany to continue what had been started here. Hell, he could probably pay Hans enough to go with him for a couple of weeks. Money was money, and he had enough for two lifetimes.

He'd actually come within a breath of making the offer. But

the thought of Catherine…He couldn't walk away. Not yet. Not like before, with so many things left undecided, unspoken. All those years ago, when he'd walked away from her he'd made terrible mistakes…a whole string of them, one after the other. Of course, there weren't any rules for what he had been going through at the time, nothing to tell him what he had to do, and how he had to do it. It had been an overwhelming time in his life, giving up something he desperately wanted in order to take up something from which he'd already turned away.

He hadn't been thinking. Not for months, maybe years. Then, by the time that his life had found its groove, there'd been too many things done that couldn't be undone.

Catherine was one of them. *She'd told him she hated him.* After words like that, there was nowhere left to go. Nothing left to do. No more reasons to try because he hated himself.

But, damn it, he loved her. Then…now…Sometimes, though, love wasn't enough. If it was, Dario wouldn't have died.

As the black limousine sped down the slippery drive and disappeared through the gates, its form becoming a black speck in the falling snow, Dante turned around and walked slowly back through the clinic doors. So much of what he loved had driven away, yet so much of what he loved sat locked in an office down the hall. He wanted it all. The problem was, he didn't know how he could have it.

Or if he even deserved it.

CHAPTER TEN

IT WAS too early in the season for all this snow. It had been coming down for hours now. Steady, heavy, going from periods where it was a lighter fall to periods of near-blizzard proportions. At Aeberhard, they weren't snowed in. Far from it. This was ski country after all, and snow was welcomed. Even worshiped, in the widest sense of the word. Yet Catherine worried a little about matters like how to get the patients in and out of the facility, or what to do about medical supplies if they were cut off. She even worried if there was enough food in the storehouse to last for a period of days without a delivery, should that happen, even though they kept a well-stocked pantry.

She'd been here for the snowy season last year, but she'd paid little attention to the winter weather details as she had been so new to her position. To be honest, she wasn't even sure she remembered that much snow, that's how involved she'd been in getting used to her medical duties.

But her worries were even greater now that she was part-owner. Her responsibilities had grown. Everything fell to her—not only the medical side of operations, but every last speck and nuance of Aeberhard, from the shoveling of the walkways to the back-up generators to the supply of staple foods in storage.

She trusted the people who worked here to do their jobs. Yet she was still restless as the snow kept falling. Probably a mixture of everything piling up on her. It had been a bumpy few days after all. First, Dante coming here. Then learning the truth about her father. And the truth of her feelings for Dante. On top of that, thinking about what Max had said to her, that she didn't stand up for what she wanted. There were so many things to consider, so many things with which she had to come to terms.

No wonder she was about to jump right out of her skin. She had too much pent-up aggravation going on without an escape valve.

"So I'll make one," she said aloud, as she grabbed her coat from the peg by the door. A little walk in the snow, some nice, invigorating fresh air. That would clear her head.

Brilliant idea, Catherine thought, heading off down the hall, clutching a notebook to her chest. She was ready to work off some of her frustration by taking an inventory of non-critical medical supplies in the outermost storehouse—tongue depressors, bandages, emesis basins and a whole host of other things not vital enough to earn themselves a place in the clinic's main storage.

Just a few minutes…that's all she wanted. A few minutes away from work to think, to sort out her life and, if she was lucky, find a bit of perspective again. In these last few days it seemed like she'd lost every bit of what she'd come to count on in herself, but what was moving in to fill the void left behind scared her. Yet, oddly enough, she welcomed it.

Catherine opened the door, forced herself out into the bitter face of the wind, only to discover that the air was even colder than she'd thought it would be. The first slap of it against the little bit of her skin that was left exposed snatched away her breath, and it was several seconds before she got it back again. Still, the sting of it felt good, made her feel alive, and vital. Those were things she hadn't felt much lately. Not outside her work, anyway.

Fighting her way step by step, and taking care not to slip and fall, Catherine ducked her head to the blustery force as she pushed forward into it, its whistling shrill in her ears. She did give a brief thought to turning back, but dismissed it quickly. There was a brute, exciting power in this storm, and she, *the one who'd never risked anything in her life*, was feeling an unexpected thrill, being part of it. This was the day she dared, perhaps for the first time. And she dared only because she needed to understand how. And why.

She made it to the storehouse without any problems, spent about ten minutes engaged in what turned out to be worthless inventory-taking, as the inventory list was complete, then clicked off the light and stepped back outside, quite surprised to find how much worse the weather had become in that short time. Across the way, she could make out the form of the clinic but, with the way the snow was blowing now, not the details. It wasn't that far away, she told herself, as she started off towards the building.

Three minutes into the trudge, three that felt like thirty, she stopped to catch her breath, realizing only then that she had started this trek at the same time the blizzard had been on the verge of striking. Three minutes out and she was now in near white-out conditions. Time to return to the storehouse. Wait there. It was cozy, warm. Safe.

She spun around to return, discovering that she'd totally lost her sense of direction. The storehouse wasn't there. Nothing was there! Just white. Cold, stark white.

She was lost! Standing out in the middle of a blizzard without her bearings, and the first things that came to mind, naturally, were all those stories about people who perished in these conditions, only steps away from safety, because they simply couldn't find it.

Were they true? She didn't know, didn't want to think about it. Yet, that's all she could think of as a claw of panic reached out and ripped at her throat. She couldn't see...couldn't breathe... Her pulse hammered, creeping up from her chest to slam at her temples. Her lungs seized, constricted deep within a chest that refused to expand. The muscles in her legs began to give way.

You can do this! her brain shrieked at her, but her body fought back, wouldn't move, anchored her to the spot,

"Catherine!"

She straightened, shaking herself from the stupor trying to settle over her. Then she made herself breathe. Forced the cold air in, forced it back out. Again…again…

Don't panic!

Catherine wiped the snow from her face, brushing away the tiny ice crystals clinging to her eyelashes. When she could see again, she turned slowly in a circle, fighting to regain her bearings.

The storehouse had to be close. Think, Catherine, think!

"Catherine!"

She fought to look, but all she could see was whiteness. Everywhere. Every direction. All around her whiteness. It was exhilarating, yet frightening. She might be mere inches from a safe, protective doorway, or not. She didn't know.

Keep your head. You can do this.

Adrenalin was coursing through her body now. She could feel the tingle, the heightened awareness. Her senses were so alive, so tuned into the vast emptiness all around her. Funny how fright was not overtaking her as it should. As she'd thought it would. Was this how her father had felt on the precipice, or at the moment he jumped from an airplane? Was this what Dante felt when he stepped into his car?

Catherine shut her eyes for a moment, trying to visualize where she was, but the image of Dante popped into her mind. She did love him, but this was one hell of a time to think about it. Yet he was there, *in her mind*, standing in front of her, urging her into his arms. Calling out her name…

"Catherine!"

One step, two, three…Towards Dante, even though he wasn't there. "Dante," she whispered.

"Catherine!"

As Catherine continued to fight her way through the snow, the wind was picking up even more, a full blizzard on the verge of dumping its worst down on her. *Keep moving*, she told herself. *To Dante.* But her body was beginning to stiffen, her legs starting to balk at the steps. Yet the adrenalin kept welling up, causing her heart to pump even harder—pump so hard it was fighting back the very breath she was drawing in. Her lungs hurt, turning her breathing into a conscious effort. She had to will herself to take that breath, or collapse.

"Catherine!"

Breathe…breathe…

After a minute of struggling with her respirations, the light-headedness finally found its way in, and her toes and fingers started prickling. Her blood gases were adjusting in a fatal swing. The doctor in her realized that. Realized it as her lips went numb. Realized it as her thinking became muddled. *Have to keep going.*

"Catherine!"

Another step forward, then another, then another, then… Catherine crumpled to the ground. "Dante," she whispered. Then nothing.

He'd seen her go out, then minutes later he'd gone after her. It was time to talk, to set things straight. But she'd walked straight into a blizzard, and at the precise moment he realized that she was out in the very worst of it, all he knew was that he had to find her, and nothing else mattered. Not even the fact that the bitter cold of the snow through which he was trudging felt like icy knives stabbing through his ankle.

"Catherine!" he shouted, making slow progress into the snow, intermittently walking and calling. Then listening.

But all he heard was the wind. Even the sound of his boots crunching in the snow was blown away.

This wasn't easy, wobbling around on a bad ankle, using a cane that hindered more than helped, under conditions that even the most able-bodied would struggle against. Only a minute or two out and his ankle was already aching like somebody had sawn through it with a serrated knife. Overall, he was in good enough shape and under different circumstances this wouldn't have been such a struggle. But as he continued, pushing himself through the snow, his ankle twisted, and threatened to give out. He couldn't stop though. Something in his heart, in his soul, told him Catherine was in trouble.

Dante hadn't gone far, still fighting heavy wind and snow, when he heard it... Was that his name? Not a shout. More like a soft cry being blown towards him on the wind. He stopped again, listened, struggled to see though the falling snow, but he couldn't. So he called Catherine's name, and called again. Then continued...his steps slow and very deliberate. The wind was picking up even more now. Staying upright becoming more difficult.

He couldn't imagine how Catherine was enduring, prayed that she was, and moved on.

After an eternity, he stopped and called her name again. He didn't expect an answer, but once again he heard his name blow in on the wind. Another few steps forward, then... "Catherine!" he cried, dropping to his knees and scooping her up in his arms. He brushed the snow from her face, threw off his gloves and felt her neck for a pulse. Steady and strong. A bit fast, but not critical. "Catherine," he said, and she woke up to his voice.

She opened her eyes to nothing but white, and choked in a panicked breath. Then she flailed at the snow for a moment, not to make a graceful snow angel but to push away the snow drifting up around her. She was cold, but not paralyzingly so, which meant she hadn't been down too long. Minutes, probably. Or less.

"Catherine, are you OK?"

She felt the touch on her mittened hand. Someone tugging at her. *Dante tugging at her.* "Where are you?" she screamed into the white void.

"Here, Catherine," he said, taking hold of her other hand now and pulling her up to a sitting position.

"How did you find me?" she sputtered, spitting out a mouthful of snow.

"Saw you leave. Came after you." He gave her one final tug and she popped up to her feet, right into Dante's arms.

He wrapped his arms around her, but only for a moment, then he shouted, "We've got to get inside. It's getting worse!"

"Which way?" she called back to him, fighting her way through the daze that had come over her.

"Damned if I know for sure, but I'm guessing we're not far from one of the outbuildings. Don't know which one."

It didn't matter which one. A roof was a roof, and all the buildings were heated. "Dante, I don't know which way…"

"Hold on," he shouted, then started to move forward through the snow at a slow, steady pace, taking a step then steadying himself with his quadcane before he took another step.

Instinctively, Catherine moved in next to him to support him, and while she lent him her physical strength to plow through all this, it was his emotional support that got her through. Just knowing Dante was there with her was all she needed. She was restored, her will to move returned. And for the next minutes, as the two of then battled against the wind and struggled through the mounting drifts, holding onto each other, Catherine never once doubted the outcome. Which turned out to be one of the outbuildings. They stumbled into the side of it, groped and clawed their way around to the front and found the door.

They were safe. Alive, and safe. Tumbling inside, still clinging to each other, it was only when the door was shut behind them that he realized how close they had come out there…close to death. One misstep, veering off in a different direction…so much left to the fates. Their deaths…the fact that he'd even found her. Surviving together.

So much left to the fates indeed. Right then all he knew was that he loved her. That was part of his fate. But the rest of it…he really didn't know.

It wasn't as warm inside as she'd expected. The generator was out, but the residual heat was trapped inside the old tool shed. It was small, cramped and very dark. And blessedly safe.

Once Dante forced the door shut, Catherine finally let go of him and slumped to the floor, too exhausted to move towards the rear of the shed. She wasn't sure she could move anywhere ever again. No point in the dark. "You OK?" she asked, gasping for breath.

He didn't answer for a moment, and she was instantly alert. "Dante?" she called into the darkness, looking around, thrashing out, trying to find his form. But she couldn't even discern the shadows.

"Fine," he finally panted. "We need to get out of these wet clothes. Is there anything in here we can use to keep us warm?"

She thought for a moment. "Some old packing blankets we use when we move furniture. Don't know where."

"I'll look."

His voice was odd. Hoarse, but not weak. "Your ankle?" she asked, as she struggled out of her garments.

He didn't answer again, which was when she started to thrash out in the dark one more time, panicking, trying to find him. "Dante?" she cried. "Where are you?"

"Back here," he called from somewhere much deeper in the shed.

Now she could hear the shuffling and clanking of various

tools, hear what she thought was a very difficult gait on the cement floor. She recognized the sound of his limp, of his struggle to drag his foot. Her first horrified thought was that he might have re-broken his ankle. *To come after her!* Nausea assaulted her stomach. "Dante, sit down. I don't want you putting any more weight on your ankle."

"I'm fine," he snapped.

"No, you're not," she said, trying to sound calm, even though every last nerve in her body was rioting. He was injured. It was her fault. She'd hurt him! "Just sit down, please."

Dante didn't answer, and Catherine held her breath for a moment. Then she called out to him again. "Dante..."

In response, a light from the back snapped on. A small beam from a torch. He held it to his face and she saw the smile tweaking the corners of his mouth. "Remember that night when we had that thunderstorm? The electricity was out..."

"And you found some candles," she said, thinking back to the way that night had ended.

"And you knocked one of them over and started a fire."

In spite of herself, Catherine laughed. "Small fire. You put it out." And in doing so had started an even bigger fire between them—one that hadn't been put out so easily.

"You burned up my lab coat and my shoes."

"Good thing you weren't in them." They had been in a heap on the floor, next to her clothes. Nice memories from a very nice time in her life. The best time in her life. "Look, you really do need to come sit down."

"You're right. I do." He limped back to the front of the shed, dropped a pile of thick packing quilts down on top of Catherine, then slid to the floor next to her.

"Can I look at your ankle?" she asked.

He didn't give her permission, but neither did he protest as she eased into position and pulled off his boot, then his soggy sock. "Point that light down here," she said, beginning a gentle prod, first the inside of Dante's ankle then the outside.

So many scars from so many surgeries, and now she wasn't sure that there wouldn't be another surgical scar there soon. "Where does it hurt?" she asked.

"Nowhere in particular," he said, even though as she attempted to move his ankle in an anti-clockwise circle, he sucked in an intense gasp.

Nothing felt broken from what she could feel. Not all breaks were palpable, though. The good thing was that he still had good residual range of motion. Stiff, very painful, but good. He was trying to be brave about it, though, and she recognized the subtleties—the change in breathing patterns, the flinching of muscles. "Dante, I'm so sorry about this."

"Not your fault," he forced out, as she reversed the movement to clockwise circles.

"You came out after me. I shouldn't have started out in the first place, but..." She ran her fingers over the top of his foot, assessing each bone as she did so. Satisfied that nothing was obviously broken, her fingers wandered lightly towards his ankle. Dante sucked in a sharp breath through his teeth as she reached the tops of his toes, and Catherine automatically pulled her hand back. "Sorry," she choked.

"Not pain," he said.

"You're not gasping from pain?"

"Not everything that elicits a gasp is painful. Remember that night, after the fire?" He reached out and took her hand. "We were good together, Catherine. I think we still are. If you want us to be."

"But I can't, Dante. As much as I want it...want us...*want you*, I can't." She rid him of his other boot, then helped him struggle out of his soaked jeans. She followed suit, shedding herself of everything soggy and cold, then she spread out one of the packing quilts on the floor and pulled the other two quilts on top of them—one over Dante and one over her. Two quilts that kept them decently separated. "I'll need to get some X-rays of your ankle when we get back into the clinic, but I don't think you've done any permanent damage. I didn't feel any broken bones, the tendons felt fine and there was no swelling. You may have a nasty twist, but I don't think you've done anything to set back your progress too much."

"Always the doctor, aren't you, Catherine?" he snapped.

"And what else am I supposed to be?" she cried.

"Catherine Brannon. The Catherine Brannon I met all those years ago."

"Not any more, Dante. She's gone."

"Are you sure?"

Was she sure? She'd worked hard to put that Catherine away. But, no, she wasn't sure she'd succeeded, although she wouldn't admit that to him. Oh, it would be easy to tumble into his arms right now. They were practically naked under the quilts—a perfect scenario, and one she wanted on so many levels. It would be easy to lift her quilt and invite him in. The two of them, trapped in a tool shed in a blizzard, passing the time by making love. Nice romantic fantasy, and one so easy to slip into. But what about tomorrow, and the day after, and the day after that, when the blizzard was over, and the toolshed was no longer a romantic little hideaway, and Dante was still Dante, and she was still who she was? What then? "I'm very sure she's gone. I've spent a lot of time trying to put her away. She needs to stay where she is."

"I don't believe that, Catherine. What I think is that you're the same person you've always been. The same amazing person I met years ago."

"Amazing perhaps, and wiser for sure," she said on a sigh. "Especially these past few days."

"So why do I get the impression that you're fighting yourself?"

"Maybe because I am. Wanting something, wishing for it to happen yet knowing I can't have it…"

"But I love you, Catherine," he whispered. "I always have, and that hasn't changed."

"And love's never enough." She felt the tears welling in her eyes. This wasn't the way she'd wanted to end it…end it for ever this time. Not in a tool shed. Not in a blizzard. But it would end here now because the ugly truth was that, she couldn't make it work with Dante. As much as she wanted to, there wasn't enough in her to hold onto him. Wanting and having were two vastly different things, and in the end she was only Catherine Brannon, the one who stood on the outside looking in, never being allowed in.

"Do you hate what I do that much?" he asked, his voice sounding strained.

"Hate. Fear. Does it matter? We don't work, so wouldn't it simply be easier walking away, leaving it alone? Before we go further? Before we say or do something…cause more pain?" She shook her head. "Because I don't want to hurt you, Dante. I never want to hurt you, but I will."

"You owe me more than this, Catherine." His voice was bitter now. "You owe me an explanation. I need to understand this!"

How could he when she didn't? "Like I needed to understand why you walked out on me the first time?" she snapped, truly regretting what she'd said. But she had to. It was the only way to put emotional distance between them. "Where were you *telling me* what I needed to hear then, Dante?"

He was quiet for a moment, and she heard him draw in a ragged breath. It sounded like stark pain and she was glad the shed was dark because seeing Dante's face would have broken her heart. Could she have found the courage to do this while looking at his beautiful face?

She hated this, hated herself for dragging out the raw feelings. But she loved him, and he loved her. It was a fatal love, though, and she loved Dante far too much to let her inadequacies into his life. He was right. She did owe him, and pushing him away from her was the high price she would pay for that love. What she owed Dante was the happiness her father had never found with his family and the trust that wasn't in her. "Where was the explanation you owed me then?" she continued. "When I didn't know, and you weren't telling me, and I was left guessing, and wondering?"

"You'd shut me out, told me to go away. Told me you hated me. What the hell did you expect me to do?"

"Fight for me, Dante. I wanted you to want me so much that you'd fight for me."

"But there was no fight, Catherine. I don't understand."

"There was always a fight, Dante. You just didn't know what it was. Then when you left and changed so many things in our relationship…" The shallow breath she drew in trembled. "And you didn't even tell me they were changing."

"But I didn't want us to change," he said, the anger now abating.

"Yes, you did. What we had, it worked for who we were. Then, all of a sudden, you changed the rules."

"Because the rules in my life changed, Catherine. I didn't have any control over that. With my family situation—my father's heart attack, unresolved issues after Dario's death, then with your situation…"

"I wasn't part of a situation, Dante. I was part of a relationship, and you forgot that. I was a decision, a problem to solve."

"No," he whispered.

"Yes. And I did hate you for a while when you called and told me what you'd decided to do, and that laundry list of decisions affecting your life included me—after I'd already heard my destiny on a television sports broadcast."

"Too many pressures, Catherine. I'm sorry. I wasn't…" He

paused, struggling to find the right words. "I'm sorry I wasn't faithful to you."

She was a movie star, and it had made the news. It had hurt, but no more so than anything else going on between them. "We weren't engaged any longer. It didn't matter."

"It did, Catherine. To me, it did. Things got complicated, and there's no excuse for what happened. I was reacting to so many things. Angry. You'd said you hated me."

Catherine laughed bitterly. "So you used that as an excuse to climb into another woman's bed the instant we separated? I couldn't come to you so you turned to someone else?"

"It wasn't like that."

"It's always like that, Dante. Mistresses come in different forms, different seductions. And there's no way to fight that. Believe it or not, I do understand and I'm not angry with you about that." That was the truth, too. There had been too many things going on, too many wild, uncontrolled emotions. She'd reacted by telling him she hated him, he'd reacted with another woman. They'd driven each other to what they'd done.

"No, Catherine," he snarled, "you don't understand. You don't understand a damned thing!"

"Because you didn't trust me enough to help me understand, Dante."

"But you kept your distance, didn't want to be let in. You never let me in. And you were the one who set the rules, Catherine. Not me."

Her rules. He was right about that. She had kept her distance. That's all she knew how to do. "Sometimes it's easier that way."

"Why?" he asked.

"Because the closer you get, the more you hurt. People let you down, or you let them down. Either way, the pain is inevitable." And unbearable.

"Like the way I hurt Dario," he whispered, almost under this breath.

"I don't understand," she said, hearing the pain in his voice.

"Neither did Dario, and that's the last thing he ever said to me, that he didn't understand why I'd broken a promise to him." Dante's voice was filled with an anguish like she'd never before heard—an anguish that was ripping at her heart. "He was in the points for the championship. This was the race that would have put Dario at the top, and I was supposed to be there with him. I'd promised, and we'd planned it for weeks, then I backed out at the last minute. Told him I couldn't make it, that there would be other races and other championships. And the hell of it was there was no reason for me not to go. I was just tired. That's all. Too damned tired."

"I'm so sorry," she whispered, wishing she had other words, better words, words that could help ease his pain. But she didn't, and she felt inadequate.

"I'd been to every other race Dario had asked me to come and watch, and there were so many races over the years. I just didn't want to go and that's what I told him. He was hurt. Angry. And still getting over the death of his wife."

He paused for a moment, and everything in the shed went so quiet she could almost hear the snow coming down outside. It was an eerie silence, one so charged with sadness and regret that it caused her to shiver. "You couldn't have known…"

"But I should have. That's the thing! I should have known what an emotional wreck he was, Catherine. We were twins, for God's sake. Twins have that connection…Dario and I had that connection. But I didn't know. Or I didn't want to know."

"I don't believe that."

"Well, do. I was too involved," he continued on. "I'd taken too much time off from the hospital after my sister-in-law's death, and my position was in jeopardy. Which is ironic, isn't it, seeing how I didn't follow through on being a doctor anyway? Then I argued with him, told him my career was in jeopardy. But I should have known…should have sensed that the real jeopardy was his. And my last words to my brother…I told him he needed to live his life and leave me alone to live mine. He told me he didn't understand what was going on with me, why I was doing this, and I hung up on him."

"Why were you doing it?" she asked gently.

He shuddered in a breath. "I loved him, and I wasn't jealous, but I was just tired and I needed a break from the family. That's all it was."

No wonder he hadn't told her, blaming himself the way he had. "He knew you loved him, Dante. It was a tough time for all of you, he understood that. You loved each other, and nothing, not even your argument, changed that." She felt so inadequate, so utterly useless, because she understood the terrible grief of never, *ever* making it right with someone. Understood it so well. "We all say things we regret." She had said so many hateful things to her father. "That's part of loving someone, I think. They get the best of us, and also the worst."

"But my worst killed my brother! He needed me, and I turned my back on him."

"No," she choked, reaching across for Dante's hand. But he jerked away from her. "You're wrong. And Dario would be the first one to tell you that."

"How can you know that, Catherine? How could anybody know that? He was upset about losing Louisa, which caused a break in his concentration. And I could have stopped him from driving. But I was too busy being the selfish bastard you accused me of being."

More than anybody else could, she did understand. "Dante," she said gently, trying to take hold of his hand again. This time he let her, but his body was stiff, resistant. "I'm sorry. I didn't mean that. It was just another of those bad reactions we both seem to have with each other. And Dario's death was a terrible tragedy, nobody's to blame. He made his choice."

"And it wasn't a good choice."

"But it was his choice, Dante. *His.* He deserved the respect of being allowed to make his own choice."

"Which got him killed."

"A slippery track got him killed. The reports said a little oil combined with the water on that curve would have been a deadly combination for anyone hitting that spot. I did read the newspapers about it. That was the official verdict."

"But if he hadn't been on the track in the first place…"

"You can't make other people's choices for them, Dante. That's not your right. I think Dario would have driven no matter what you did." You couldn't make other people's decisions for them, and you couldn't allow them to make decisions for you. It was a tangled reality, and one she hadn't gotten right herself because she'd spent a lifetime allowing so many people to make her decisions. And suddenly she understood. It was crystal clear.

Catherine scooted closer to Dante until they were touching. Still under separate quilts, but together. Then she threw off her own quilt and snuggled under Dante's. His body was warm against hers. But his muscles were still tight. Unyielding. "I didn't know Dario, Dante, but he was your twin and if he was anything like you, I know he would have never put other lives in jeopardy because he was having a bad day. He would have stepped away from the car, the way you would." She smiled as she snuggled her head into his shoulder. "The way any good Baldassare would."

He lifted his arm to wrap it around her shoulder. "You might think that but the truth is we'll never know."

"Yes, Dante. We do know. You may not be ready to forgive yourself yet, but deep in your heart you know."

What Catherine knew was that she shouldn't be doing this. Shouldn't be under the same quilt with him, pressed to his body, his arm around her. But it was her choice, truly her choice because she couldn't be anywhere else, doing anything else right then. She did love Dante, but nothing had changed about what she had to do. Except when she would do it. Not now. Not in the tool shed. Not in the blizzard. Like Dante had never been able to forgive himself for arguing with Dario when he had, she would never be able to forgive herself for ending it with Dante at this moment. "Dante, I…"

She meant to apologize again but before the words were out his fingers were caressing a trail up her bare arm. Instantly, her breathing went shallow and her heart rate doubled. In a wave of turbulent emotion, knowing what was to come and wanting it like she'd never wanted anything in her life, Catherine did the opposite of what she'd expected to do. She pulled away from Dante. Scooted to the edge of the quilt underneath them until she had no top quilt on at all, then fumbled around in the dark for it.

"I have it," he said, his voice so low it nearly blended into the darkness. "And I'll be glad to share it with you."

"I'm fine," she lied, already starting to shiver. She was down to bra and panties, the only dry clothes she'd had left when she'd rid herself of the top wet layers.

"It's cold out there."

"It's warm enough." She wouldn't die of exposure or anything like that, but there was nothing about her that was close to being warm. Still, to crawl back under the quilt with Dante would be to surrender to something she was desperately trying to fight in the only way she knew how.

"Does it frighten you that much, Catherine? Because if it does, all you have to do is say no, and I'll respect your wishes. I won't lay a hand on you."

"Yes, it does frighten me, Dante. Because I want this, want you. And I can't…"

Before she could finish, she felt the warm rush of the blanket come down on her, and with it Dante. "No?" he asked.

"Yes," she whispered. "Please, yes."

Instantly, Dante moved his hand to her hip, slipping his fingers under her panties, his fingertips dancing their way across her lower belly, then down.

Catherine arched under him, trying to take in a deep calming breath, but as his fingers continued their waltz into places that hadn't been touched this way since he'd last touched her there, all she could do was surrender to the pants and gasps he was purposely trying to elicit from her. Her body was responding too quickly to suppress anything, try as she may. Just a mere touch and a small whimper escaped her lips, then crescendoed into a moan. He'd always known how, and she'd always been so fast to react... "Dante!" she cried, her voice now loud and hoarse.

He chuckled as she rocked against his hand, then bent to kiss her between her breasts when she relaxed. "I always loved the way you did that," he said, reaching round to remove her bra.

"And I always loved the way you did *that*," she purred in response. It was their first time again. Everything exciting and new. So much to explore. Yet this time so familiar.

"Remember what I used to say?" he asked.

"That my body was meant to be touched?"

"The perfect body to touch," he said, removing her panties and tracing a delicate line from the valley between her breasts to the valley below. "To taste, to hold..." He pulled her to him now, lowering his lips to hers. But gently. Only for a moment, though, as her tongue found his, arousing a crazy fluttering in her belly and a fire even lower.

"Dante," she cried urgently, as she wrapped her legs around him, not ashamed of the pounding need overtaking her that was driving out sense. It should have been slower—old lovers reuniting. They should have taken their time to explore, to savor this first and very last time, but her need to have him inside her, to be one with him once more, shoved everything else out of her mind, and in that instant, as she opened herself to him, she felt his body tense, then that first hard stroke of him robbed her of breath.

He slid his hands down her back and when he'd reached her bottom, pulled her harder into him, as if even a hair's-breadth between them was too much to bear. There he held her there for a moment, while she felt the heat of him course through her, and smelt the pure male sex invade her in a way she'd never thought she would have again. "I do love you," she whispered, as she began to thrust.

His response was a deep, guttural moan, and something that sounded like an apology. But she couldn't tell for sure because he began to ride the motion she'd created, first merely going along then finally dominating. Moving together, the feel of his chest rubbing over her breasts, each of his thrusts becoming harder and harder…Catherine melted into the pure pleasure of it all, grabbing hold of Dante's shoulders to find her own wild rhythm. It was different this time. Harder. More urgent. For her a release of so many years and emotions… "Dante," she gasped as she reached her climax. Which drove him to his. For those moments there were no years between them. No years, no problems, no reality but their own.

Then, suddenly, that's all there was. Years of separation. Once it was over, Dante pulled away, taking his quilt with him. He dressed, and went to sit on the other side of the shed. And Catherine scooted to her side of the quilt and stayed huddled there until the blizzard abated, and they were able to go back to the clinic.

The next morning, Catherine was gone. That's the only way she could do this—to leave. Go home to go figure out the pieces of her life and see what could be salvaged. And what couldn't.

CHAPTER ELEVEN

Five months later

SHE looked in the full-length mirror, turned from side to side, then spun away from the mirror for a quick glance over her shoulder at the back view. Not too bad. She wasn't showing much yet. Not so much that anyone who didn't know she was pregnant would notice. Except Max. He knew, and he was keeping track of every pound she gained, calling himself the baby's grandfather, making sure she took her proper prenatal vitamins, ate the proper foods, got the proper rest.

Dante didn't know yet. Which was why she was here, to tell him. Oh, it would have been easy enough to stay quiet about it, to be conveniently evasive for the next eighteen years or so, and end up being like the women in the romance novels who had secret babies. But she wasn't the kind of woman who would do that. Dante's child was growing inside her. He was a marvelous father already, and he had the right to know he would soon be a father again.

Today she would tell him, then let him make his choices as she'd already made hers.

Laying her hand on her still nearly flat belly, she smiled. She truly loved this choice.

Telling Dante was the right thing to do, she told herself all the way to the race course. Her plan was to tell him he was going to be a father in four more months, then let the rest of it happen as it may. After that time in the shed, and the way he'd turned away from her, she felt certain he would be glad to be rid of the tie to her. He'd told her he loved her, and she didn't think he'd lied about it. Dante wouldn't do that. But he'd pulled away from her like almost everybody else in her life had done, which was why she'd made the choice she had—to keep her child.

Her choice. And nothing in her life had ever made her happier.

She rubbed her belly again, trying to feel the swell of it through her cotton sweater. She wanted to get fat, wanted to see her body puff out in ways some women moaned about.

It was an amazing thing, really. She hadn't even known she was pregnant. And her a doctor. She'd thought it was stress. Thought she was working too hard. Thought…well, she wasn't sure what else she'd thought, but when she'd bought that little home pregnancy kit and tested herself just six weeks ago, her life had definitely changed. Now it was about to change again, and she was scared.

Buck up, she thought as she climbed out of the taxi an hour later. *You can do this.* She had everything. A marvelous job at Aeberhard, Max as a wonderful mentor and friend, Dante's son…"You can do this," she whispered, as she walked towards the entrance. Bahrain. She'd come a long way to do this and there was no turning back now.

As thousands of spectators flowed to the race track, sweeping Catherine along with them, she was amazed by the sheer size of the event. People everywhere packing in, people with Dante's name on their lips. She heard it, heard their admiration for him.

Admittedly, this track was impressive—the ten-story VIP tower she could see off in the distance, all the sponsor's signs, the sleek design of the seats. The race course had been built in a rolling desert, right alongside a camel farm. Today Sakhir, one of the largest of Bahrain's thirty-six islands, was fairly buzzing with activity, and Catherine felt the excitement tingling around her all the way to her seat. She paused for a moment before she sat down to listen to a small crowd chanting Dante's name.

"Dante! Dante! Dante!"

Admittedly, she felt a swell of pride over that. The man she loved…the father of her baby was beloved. People flocked in from all around the world to see him.

Yes, it had taken her a while to gather the courage to come. Even after she had decided to make the trip, there had been no tickets available, no hotel rooms. An easy excuse to back out. But Max had pulled some strings. He knew someone who had the right connections. So now here she was, getting ready to watch Dante drive. She hadn't had a change of heart about that. Not in the sense that she'd become a fan of any sport where there were so many risks. But something had happened when she'd discovered she was pregnant, carrying a son—she'd had a gradual awakening. This baby inside her might be like his father. Gianni was. And for the Baldassare family, heredity had a strong hold. Coming here was coming to terms, was loving Dante, but most of all was loving her baby. To love meant to support and by doing this she was learning how. All this would be part of her son's life. Or his entire life. *To love was to support*. At long last, it was time.

Would it make any difference in her relationship with Dante? Honestly, she didn't know. But for now, one thing at a time. Telling Dante about his child was the priority.

"Ma'am," a man standing in the aisle of the grandstand said, gesturing to Catherine. He wore a security guard's uniform, and briefly she wondered if she'd come to the wrong seat and he was there to take her away

"Would you come with me?"

She looked around, first over her left shoulder, then her right, positive he must be speaking to someone else. But he wasn't. "Excuse me," she said, immediately checking her ticket to make sure she'd come to the correct seat. She had. "This is my seat," she said, holding out the ticket for him to inspect.

He nodded. "I understand, but I still need you to follow me."

Reluctantly, Catherine stood, then followed the man out of the grandstand, where he had a small motor cart waiting to take her somewhere else. "My passport is in order," she said.

"I'm sure it is," he replied.

"Then can you tell me where you're taking me? And why?"

He smiled but didn't answer, and by the time he stopped the motor cart in an area well away from the roar of the crowd, Catherine was nervous. Until she saw Gianni. He was already running to her by the time she'd climbed out of the cart, and she had barely bent down for his embrace when he jumped into her arms. "Papa let me sit in his car!" he cried. "He said I can drive it someday!"

Gianni was her baby's brother. It had just occurred to her that this little boy she'd come to love totally would be her son's older brother. There was so much of Dante in him and she had no doubt there would be so much of Dante in her child. "When did this happen?" she said, as Gianni pulled her by the hand along a line of garages for the race cars. This bloodline—it did frighten her. But it was part of her now.

"This morning. He said he had all kinds of surprises for me, and that was to be the first one."

"What was the second one?" she enquired, looking around to see if she could catch sight of Dante. She wasn't going to tell him until after the race, and while she truly did believe what she'd said months ago, that Dario wouldn't have stepped into his car had he been distracted by the argument he'd had with Dante, she wasn't about to risk distracting Dante with this news. To be honest, she didn't know how he would take it. He was so wonderful with Gianni that she imagined he would be excited. But there was a chance he would hate having a permanent tie to her.

So that news would wait.

"There isn't a second one yet. Papa said it would be waiting for me after the race today."

"So why did that security guard bring me here?" she asked, as they made their way through a cluster of reporters with video cameras and microphones to one particular garage where there seemed to be more activity than in any of the others.

"I think Papa wanted to see you," he said quite innocently.

"He knew I was coming?"

Gianni shrugged. "Maybe that was my second surprise." He smiled. "You'd be a good surprise, but I was hoping for a puppy."

Catherine laughed. She dearly loved Gianni and she prayed his new little brother would be just like him, Baldassare enthusiasm, Baldassare risks, and all. "Well, if Dante doesn't get you a puppy, and he'll allow you to have one, perhaps I'll find you a puppy, if that's OK."

Gianni's response to that was to call out to one of his friends in the crowd that he was getting a puppy, then run off, leaving Catherine standing there wondering what to do next.

"Lost?" the familiar voice came from over her shoulder.

She spun around to face him. "How did you know I'd be here?" she asked, trying not to sound breathless. But she was. She loved this man and after so many months of thinking nothing could ever come of it, she was finally willing to see what could happen. Another choice, solely hers. And if he said no, if anything other than the son they shared was not to be, it would not be because she'd stood off to the side and let it.

"I have my ways," he said, chuckling. He eyes raked over her, head to toe, then back up again.

"Max?" Now it made sense. His connection to get her a ticket and a room had been Dante. The dear old sneak! "Am I part of Gianni's surprise, by any chance? Were you and Max planning this?"

"Let's just say Max and I have kept in touch."

Suddenly she wondered how much they'd kept in touch, how much Max had told him. About the baby?

"To be honest, I'm surprised you'd want to come to a race, the way you feel about such things. I'd thought about getting you to Tuscany later in the season, but never to a race track."

"I, um…I had some time off," she lied. "I've always heard Bahrain was a lovely place to visit, and—"

"And as it happens, I have a race here that coincides with your holiday. Amazing how life works out, isn't it?"

Actually, it was, and he didn't know the half of it. Unconsciously, Catherine ran her hand over her belly. "I wanted to see," she admitted. And that was true. She did. As the mother of a Baldassare, she needed to know. Needed to start her adjustment to the rest of her life.

"Look, about that day in the shed…"

Catherine held up her hand to stop him. "There's nothing to say, Dante."

"I shouldn't have…"

She shook her head. "Think about your race. Right now, that's all there is."

"Will you be here later? So we can talk?"

"I'd like that."

Dante nodded, then bent to give Catherine a polite kiss on the cheek. "I'm glad you're here," he whispered in her ear.

"Me, too," she said, almost shyly, wondering if she dared hope for anything.

As it turned out, Catherine sat with Marco in the better seats. Along with Cristofor and all three of Dante's sisters, his mother, his grandfather, some uncles, cousins and about a dozen other Baldassares she'd yet to put names to. They were an exuberant bunch. Loud, happy. Cheering Dante on, waving flags, jumping up and down every time he passed their seats. The way she should be, the way she wanted to be.

At first she was reserved, watching the cars speed by so fast she barely had time to focus on them. The roar of the engines fascinated her, she had to admit. The whines as the cars changed gear for the various curves, and this course did have some sharp ones, according to Marco, was amazing. Marco had mentioned that coming out of turn six and going straight into turn seven was a challenge, but she couldn't see that from where they were sitting, which was probably a good thing, because even as Dante passed by on the straightway in front of her, her heart always leapt to her throat.

Several times, as he held the lead, and another car got into position to pass him, Catherine did shut her eyes. But several times she kept them open too, wondering whether if she and her mother had gone to support her father in his various endeavors, it might have made a difference. Dante had so much support, so much love here…

So she watched, sharing binoculars with Marco, being coached by him on finer points of the sport she did not pretend to understand, until at one point the whole Baldassare family jumped up screaming and shouting. Then she heard it announced. Dante Baldassare had won the race. That's when she jumped up, with the rest of them, waving the Baldassare flag Marco had handed her, screaming, in English, the same things Dante's family was screaming in Italian. Catherine thought about her father for a moment, as she'd thought of him so often these past months. She did understand now, as her child was waiting to come into the world. It was about loving and protecting that child the best way you knew how. What her father had always done.

Lifting her flag above her heard, she looked up at the blue skies overhead. Part of her cheers were for him, too.

"You liked the race?" Dante asked, stepping out of the shower in his hotel suite. He was dressed in well-worn jeans and a white cotton shirt. Barefoot. Wet hair. So handsome he took her breath away.

"It was…exciting," she admitted. "In places. Better than I thought,"

"My father told me you watched a good bit of it…" he smiled "…with your hands over your eyes."

"It scares me, Dante. You know that."

"But I'm glad you came. It meant a lot to me, having you there."

"I wasn't sure you'd want me here," she said. "After the way we parted, and after what I've been reading about you." Catherine nodded almost shyly. "I know I don't have a place here, but I had to come."

I'm glad you did," he said simply. "Max said you went home for a while?"

She nodded again. "I had some things I needed to figure out. Some questions I needed to ask my mother."

"About your father?"

"About my relationship with him. I thought it might help my relationship with you if I understood my father better."

"Do you think I'm like your father?"

"Not at all. But it's taken me some time to realize that, because he lived such a big life, too."

She looked around at the suite. It was large, plush, with French antiques, all white and gold and expensive. Catherine chose a tiny chair near the door, from where she could make a quick escape if she embarrassed herself any more than she already had by coming here. Her ankles were swelling a bit now, the heat of the day finally getting to her, and she was tired. "Excuse me," she said, as she lowered herself onto the gold and white upholstery. "It's been a long day."

"Are you OK?" he asked, starting across the room in her direction.

"Water, please," she gasped, exhaustion overtaking her. Her head was starting to spin a little.

Dante left the room, then returned moments later with a glass of water. But rather than handing it to her, he held it to her lips. "Why did you come, Catherine?" he asked. "After all these months with no contact from you, without you returning my calls or answering my emails—and I did try to contact you—why did you come?"

She was almost too tired to tell him. She wanted to, needed to, but this wasn't the way she'd pictured it in her mind. In that scenario she was strong, resolute. But right now she was limp. And Dante's son, even though he wasn't so far along yet, was giving her a few good kicks. "Could I use your restroom?" she asked, instead of answering him.

Once in the bathroom, Catherine splashed some water on her face, then looked at herself in the rococo-gilt mirror. She looked like hell. That's the only way she could describe herself. Messed hair, red, sunburnt face, puffy eyes…hell. And she felt like hell, too. Possibly the best thing to do would be to tell him the news, then get out of there. Go back to her room, go to bed, and deal with it all tomorrow after he'd had time to absorb the facts.

"You OK in there?" Dante called.

She opened the door and came face to face with him. "I'm…" She felt faint again. "I'm fi—" She shut her eyes for a moment as her world started to spin around, and the next thing she knew she was in Dante's arms, on her way to his bed.

The next thing she knew after that was that it was the middle of the night, and Dante was sleeping in a chair near the bed. His head had dropped to his chest, his feet were propped up on another chair, and all she could think was that she hoped her son looked exactly like that.

"You're awake," he murmured, sitting straight up in the chair.

"How long did I sleep?" she asked, looking at the clock next to the bed.

He glanced over at the same clock. "Fourteen hours now."

"It's morning?"

"Almost." He turned on the light by the chair and pushed the hair back from his face.

"And you slept there all night."

"Some of it. I started out…"

A rolling wave of nausea came over her and she bolted from the bed and ran for the bathroom. Morning sickness. She still got it this late in her pregnancy. Normal, according to her doctor. Only an adjustment of her hormones.

Once inside, she vomited into the toilet. Twice. Her usual. Then she rinsed out her mouth and laid her hand on the doorknob. It was time. No putting it off now. Pulling open the door, she found Dante standing there like he had last night. Only this time the expression on his face was unreadable.

"The question you asked me last night," she said, pushing past him. "Why I came to the race?" She plodded back to the bed and dropped down on it. "I came to tell you I'm pregnant. And to be honest, I don't know if that comes as a shock to you, or if Max has already told you."

"Pregnant?" he asked, his face totally devoid of expression.

She studied him for a moment, expecting a reaction. But nothing. Stupid her. Somewhere in her delusional mind she'd played out this scenario so many ways. He was happy, he was angry. He would pull her into his arms and profess undying love, he would open the door and tell her to leave. But never had she expected *nothing* from Dante. He was a man who reacted. He came from a family who reacted. Yet he was not. "Pregnant," she said, fighting to adopt the same lack of expression he wore. "We weren't careful that night in the shed and—"

"No abortion," he said flatly. "Or adoption. I know you don't want children, but I do. I want this baby, Catherine. Even if you don't."

"What?" She choked in surprise.

"I said, I *want* this baby. You don't have to raise it, you don't have to be responsible for it. I will. But, please, don't get rid of it."

"Dante, I wouldn't—" She shook her head. "I want this baby! In my whole life I've never wanted anything as badly as I do this child." This child, and Dante. "Why do you think I'd even consider—?"

"Because you told me there's no room in your life for a family. That you didn't want a typical family life or children. You said you got out of your marriage before you did something foolish, like having a child."

"With my first husband," she whispered. "I didn't want those things *with him*."

Dante didn't say anything for a little while. Instead, he paced the room, from the entry door to the window on the opposite side then back again. Finally, after several minutes, he stopped in front of the bed. "But you kept telling me you loved me, yet it wouldn't work."

Catherine shut her eyes for a moment. This had not been part of any of her scenarios, but it was time for this, too. She did love him. It was going to be difficult, but he had to understand. "When I was a girl, I idolized my father. To me, he was larger than life. Everything he did was wonderful. But he pushed me away, Dante. No matter what I did, he pushed me away. Rejected me. And the more he rejected me, the more I tried to please him. But I always failed.

"And my mother did the same thing. At least in my young mind, when I saw her crying all the time and shutting herself in her room, I thought it was about me. It's easy to get detached when everyone you love doesn't love you back. I became…compliant. Do whatever they wanted and maybe they'd love me. Let them make my decisions, tell me what to do and maybe my father would be my father again."

"Build up the wall around yourself before you got hurt. Dear

God, Catherine," Dante choked. "It was never about my racing, was it?"

Catherine shook her head. "Easy excuse, and it took me a long time to figure it out. There were so many layers to peel away, and they were painful."

"After my father's heart attack, when I went home and changed my life without letting you know…"

"And expecting me to be a part of it," she added. "That's all I ever wanted, Dante. To be a part of it."

"But I wouldn't let you, and it was like your father rejecting you all over again. Catherine, I'm so sorry."

"You couldn't have known, Dante, because I didn't know. I'd never stopped being that little girl trying to get her daddy's attention any way she could. I've told myself so many things, been angry, been hurt, been indifferent. In the end my father died and I didn't make it right with him, and I suppose that was the ultimate rejection. He went away and I never had his love. All those years of being the compliant, good little girl wasted."

"And you saw that in me?"

"In some ways, yes. My father was documentary film maker, an adventurer, Dante. He climbed mountains, raced speedboats, jumped out of airplanes…people paid him to do those things and film it. And sponsors endorsed him for the risks he took. Much like the way people sponsor you to race."

Dante came to the bed and sat down next to Catherine, taking her hand into his. "I didn't know. You never told me."

"Because the first time we were together, those kinds of things didn't matter. I didn't want them to matter because I was afraid of them. It seems I've built up this brilliant way of avoiding the obvious, then rearranging what I can't avoid." She smiled sadly. "All those things should have mattered because I knew from the start I was falling in love with you. But to say them out loud meant to risk rejection. You see, by the time I was ten, I'd totally shut out my father. I hated him. Told him so on so many occasions. Hate the man then his rejection wouldn't hurt so much. Hate Dante, then his rejection wouldn't hurt so much. Reject first so I wouldn't be rejected. That's why I snapped at you that day about Gianni. I know what it's like to be the child of someone who might die the way Gianni's father did, or the way my father did. My father shut me out because he loved me and didn't want me to get hurt if he was killed. He pushed me away for what he thought was my own good, and when I saw Gianni, who so adored you, that's all I could think of…the way I adored my father, and how his lifestyle took that away. It broke my heart for Gianni since he'd already suffered a loss that I truly understand. And it broke my heart for me because I'd lost so much, too."

"Your father died because…?"

"Climbing accident. His greatest passion. He'd had a near miss or two before, but this time he was on a rockface in Utah. He got part way up and slipped. But it didn't kill him right away. He lived nearly a year as a quadriplegic before an infection overcame him. And my mother cried every day then. I was only sixteen, and during that year I hated my father for what he'd done to us, and I wouldn't go near him. He died thinking…" She slapped angrily at the tears streaming down her face. "He died thinking I didn't love him, when I always did, and I broke his heart, Dante. Which is why you've got to know that I've always loved you. From that very first day."

Dante pulled Catherine into his arms and held her tight. "Once you told me that Dario knew I loved him, I've thought about that so many times these past months. Thought about it until I realized you were right. We do things we later regret to the people we love, but in the end the love doesn't go away. It's taken me a long time to come to terms with Dario's death, but you helped me see that the fight between us didn't matter. He always knew how I felt. And your father always knew how you felt, Catherine. He knew you loved him, which is why he pushed you away… because you loved him so desperately and he didn't want to hurt you. It was his choice, and I'm sure that in that last year of his life he knew your heart was breaking like his was, too."

Catherine shuddered a sob. "When I fell in love with you, you were safe. Then you went away and became a race driver, and you weren't. But I couldn't stop loving you, Dante. I wanted to. I even thought if I married someone else it might help, but it only made the pain worse because he wasn't you." She sniffled. "I wanted to get over you, Dante. I honestly tried. But I couldn't."

He chuckled. "And that's a bad thing?"

She rubbed her belly. "No," she whispered. "No, it's not."

"I can give up the racing, Catherine. If that will make you feel better. Take away the stress."

She shook her head as she swiped at her tear again. "No. You can't. Don't you understand? That's who you are. Part of the man I fell in love with. You have to be who you are." She relaxed against his chest. "My mother always told me to never marry a man like my father, but when I went home she also told me she wouldn't have had her life any other way. But my mother isn't a strong woman. She wasn't able to cope with what it took to be married to my father, which is why I didn't get everything from her that I needed. Everything she had was for him, and she loved him desperately. But I've got more than that, Dante. So much more, if you want it."

"I do want it, Catherine. All of it."

"Are you sure? Because until you came to Aeberhard, I turned all the emotion in on my work. That wouldn't reject me. It was safe. It was an excuse, just like hating your racing was an excuse. I had to have those excuses, Dante. They were the only things that propped me up, and knowing all that doesn't mean it will be easy for me to change."

"I'll help you," he said. "And you'll help me to include you in everything I am and everything I have. That's all I want. Catherine. But I'm a Baldassare and we're…"

"Overbearing?"

"Sometimes."

"Larger than life?"

"Sometimes."

"Passionate?"

"Always."

In his arms, she sighed contentedly. "True love, Dante, is not making someone change who they are but loving them enough to support them. A very wise man once told me that, and I didn't listen well enough at the time. But he's reminded me a few times these past months…"

"I want to marry you, Catherine."

"And I want to marry you, Dante."

"No fears?"

"Always fears, but not about being rejected. You're not my father. You wouldn't do that. Not to me, not to Gianni, not to our child."

"So what do we do?"

She drew in a quivering breath. "Make compromises. You go off to your races, and I'll bring your sons to watch, but otherwise keep them home with me and have a normal family."

"Sons?" he asked. His voice cracked.

"Gianni. And Dario. Dario Emil Baldassare. Named for the two men we've loved and lost. And I have an idea that our son, being a Baldassare the way he is, as well as a Brannon, will have your blood, as well as my father's. He'll be a real risk-taker, I think. True to his nature. And I'm getting used to the idea. Or, trying to. But I'll need help."

"You'll have help. And you'll be fine, because our son's mother is quite a risk-taker herself," Dante said.

"You're not a risk, Dante. I can't promise you that I won't be nervous about your driving, or about what Gianni and Dario will eventually want to do, but I will support you in it. And support our sons in whoever they turn out to be. Oh, and for my part in this family…Max has recently deeded over more of the clinic to me. Do you mind living in Switzerland? I know you have your home in Tuscany, but there's a nice little castle not so far away that's for sale, and I thought…"

"I'd love to come and live in Switzerland with you," he said, kissing her, but not on the lips. On the belly! "In a castle, or a tool shed. Doesn't really matter to me as long as we're together. So, let me see…Five months pregnant. If the doctor in me remembers this correctly, I can still make love to my soon-to-be bride, can't I?"

"My choice," Catherine said.

"You took the words right out of my mouth," he said, then placed a kiss on hers.

"A doctor in the family!" Marco crowed, pulling Catherine into his arms. "I've always wanted a doctor in the family." It was a change of heart for the old man, who'd hated doctors for quite a while now, but he meant it, if the smile on his face signified anything.

"Dante's going to practice medicine a little while he's at Aeberhard," Catherine warned him, well aware of his opinion of doctors in general.

Marco nodded thoughtfully. "As well he should. Why let all that education go to waste?"

"But I thought…" Dante started, but Catherine laid a warning hand on his arm. It was best leaving well enough alone. Especially today of all days.

"We'll take our holidays in Tuscany," she said, feeling a little guilty over being the one to split the Baldassare family up. But Dante was fine with it, and that's all that mattered.

"And we'll take ours in Switzerland," Marco replied enthusiastically. "Long holidays to come and see my grandson!"

"Grandsons," Dante corrected him, glowing with pride.

"What?" Marco exclaimed. He blinked widely, then pulled off

his cap and threw it into the air. "The doctor is giving me another grandson? Another Baldassare?"

"Dario," she said softly.

Tears came to the old man's eyes. "Dario," he repeated, then he nodded. "He should be a great racer one day, too. Like his father." He pulled Catherine into his arms again, kissed her on the cheek, then whispered in her ear, "Or a great doctor, like both his parents."

"I'm not going to be a racer," Gianni interrupted, coming into the hotel room.

"A doctor?" Catherine asked.

He shook his head. "A downhill skier," he said resolutely. "I want to win the Olympics."

"Spoken like a true Baldassare," Catherine said, laughing as she reached out to take Dante's hand. One thing was for sure. Life with the Baldassares was going to be eventful. "Beginner hills for now," she warned Gianni.

MILLS & BOON®
Pure reading pleasure

MAY 2008 HARDBACK TITLES

ROMANCE

Bought for Revenge, Bedded for Pleasure	978 0 263 20286 1
Emma Darcy	
Forbidden: The Billionaire's Virgin Princess	978 0 263 20287 8
Lucy Monroe	
The Greek Tycoon's Convenient Wife	978 0 263 20288 5
Sharon Kendrick	
The Marciano Love-Child *Melanie Milburne*	978 0 263 20289 2
The Millionaire's Rebellious Mistress	978 0 263 20290 8
Catherine George	
The Mediterranean Billionaire's Blackmail Bargain	
Abby Green	978 0 263 20291 5
Mistress Against Her Will *Lee Wilkinson*	978 0 263 20292 2
Her Ruthless Italian Boss *Christina Hollis*	978 0 263 20293 9
Parents in Training *Barbara McMahon*	978 0 263 20294 6
Newlyweds of Convenience *Jessica Hart*	978 0 263 20295 3
The Desert Prince's Proposal *Nicola Marsh*	978 0 263 20296 0
Adopted: Outback Baby *Barbara Hannay*	978 0 263 20297 7
Winning the Single Mum's Heart	978 0 263 20298 4
Linda Goodnight	
Boardroom Bride and Groom *Shirley Jump*	978 0 263 20299 1
Proposing to the Children's Doctor	978 0 263 20300 4
Joanna Neil	
Emergency: Wife Needed *Emily Forbes*	978 0 263 20301 1

HISTORICAL

The Virtuous Courtesan *Mary Brendan*	978 0 263 20198 7
The Homeless Heiress *Anne Herries*	978 0 263 20199 4
Rebel Lady, Convenient Wife *June Francis*	978 0 263 20200 7

MEDICAL™

Virgin Midwife, Playboy Doctor	978 0 263 19894 2
Margaret McDonagh	
The Rebel Doctor's Bride *Sarah Morgan*	978 0 263 19895 9
The Surgeon's Secret Baby Wish *Laura Iding*	978 0 263 19896 6
Italian Doctor, Full-time Father *Dianne Drake*	978 0 263 19897 3

0408 Gen Std LP

Pure reading pleasure

MAY 2008 LARGE PRINT TITLES

ROMANCE

The Italian Billionaire's Ruthless Revenge *Jacqueline Baird*	978 0 263 20042 3
Accidentally Pregnant, Conveniently Wed *Sharon Kendrick*	978 0 263 20043 0
The Sheikh's Chosen Queen *Jane Porter*	978 0 263 20044 7
The Frenchman's Marriage Demand *Chantelle Shaw*	978 0 263 20045 4
Her Hand in Marriage *Jessica Steele*	978 0 263 20046 1
The Sheikh's Unsuitable Bride *Liz Fielding*	978 0 263 20047 8
The Bridesmaid's Best Man *Barbara Hannay*	978 0 263 20048 5
A Mother in a Million *Melissa James*	978 0 263 20049 2

HISTORICAL

The Vanishing Viscountess *Diane Gaston*	978 0 263 20154 3
A Wicked Liaison *Christine Merrill*	978 0 263 20155 0
Virgin Slave, Barbarian King *Louise Allen*	978 0 263 20156 7

MEDICAL™

The Magic of Christmas *Sarah Morgan*	978 0 263 19950 5
Their Lost-and-Found Family *Marion Lennox*	978 0 263 19951 2
Christmas Bride-To-Be *Alison Roberts*	978 0 263 19952 9
His Christmas Proposal *Lucy Clark*	978 0 263 19953 6
Baby: Found at Christmas *Laura Iding*	978 0 263 19954 3
The Doctor's Pregnancy Bombshell *Janice Lynn*	978 0 263 19955 0

0508 Gen Std HB

Pure reading pleasure

JUNE 2008 HARDBACK TITLES

ROMANCE

Hired: The Sheikh's Secretary Mistress *Lucy Monroe*	978 0 263 20302 8
The Billionaire's Blackmailed Bride *Jacqueline Baird*	978 0 263 20303 5
The Sicilian's Innocent Mistress *Carole Mortimer*	978 0 263 20304 2
The Sheikh's Defiant Bride *Sandra Marton*	978 0 263 20305 9
Italian Boss, Ruthless Revenge *Carol Marinelli*	978 0 263 20306 6
The Mediterranean Prince's Captive Virgin *Robyn Donald*	978 0 263 20307 3
Mistress: Hired for the Billionaire's Pleasure *India Grey*	978 0 263 20308 0
The Italian's Unwilling Wife *Kathryn Ross*	978 0 263 20309 7
Wanted: Royal Wife and Mother *Marion Lennox*	978 0 263 20310 3
The Boss's Unconventional Assistant *Jennie Adams*	978 0 263 20311 0
Inherited: Instant Family *Judy Christenberry*	978 0 263 20312 7
The Prince's Secret Bride *Raye Morgan*	978 0 263 20313 4
Milllionaire Dad, Nanny Needed! *Susan Meier*	978 0 263 20314 1
Falling for Mr Dark & Dangerous *Donna Alward*	978 0 263 20315 8
The Spanish Doctor's Love-Child *Kate Hardy*	978 0 263 20316 5
Her Very Special Boss *Anne Fraser*	978 0 263 20317 2

HISTORICAL

Miss Winthorpe's Elopement *Christine Merrill*	978 0 263 20201 4
The Rake's Unconventional Mistress *Juliet Landon*	978 0 263 20202 1
Rags-to-Riches Bride *Mary Nichols*	978 0 263 20203 8

MEDICAL™

Their Miracle Baby *Caroline Anderson*	978 0 263 19898 0
The Children's Doctor and the Single Mum *Lilian Darcy*	978 0 263 19899 7
Pregnant Nurse, New-Found Family *Lynne Marshall*	978 0 263 19900 0
The GP's Marriage Wish *Judy Campbell*	978 0 263 19901 7

® MILLS & BOON®   0508 Gen Std LP

Pure reading pleasure

JUNE 2008 LARGE PRINT TITLES

ROMANCE

The Greek Tycoon's Defiant Bride *Lynne Graham*	978 0 263 20050 8
The Italian's Rags-to-Riches Wife *Julia James*	978 0 263 20051 5
Taken by Her Greek Boss *Cathy Williams*	978 0 263 20052 2
Bedded for the Italian's Pleasure *Anne Mather*	978 0 263 20053 9
Cattle Rancher, Secret Son *Margaret Way*	978 0 263 20054 6
Rescued by the Sheikh *Barbara McMahon*	978 0 263 20055 3
Her One and Only Valentine *Trish Wylie*	978 0 263 20056 0
English Lord, Ordinary Lady *Fiona Harper*	978 0 263 20057 7

HISTORICAL

A Compromised Lady *Elizabeth Rolls*	978 0 263 20157 4
Runaway Miss *Mary Nichols*	978 0 263 20158 1
My Lady Innocent *Annie Burrows*	978 0 263 20159 8

MEDICAL™

Christmas Eve Baby *Caroline Anderson*	978 0 263 19956 7
Long-Lost Son: Brand New Family *Lilian Darcy*	978 0 263 19957 4
Their Little Christmas Miracle *Jennifer Taylor*	978 0 263 19958 1
Twins for a Christmas Bride *Josie Metcalfe*	978 0 263 19959 8
The Doctor's Very Special Christmas *Kate Hardy*	978 0 263 19960 4
A Pregnant Nurse's Christmas Wish *Meredith Webber*	978 0 263 19961 1